West Irish Folk-Tales and Romances

West Irish Folk-Tales and Romances

collected and translated

by

WILLIAM LARMINIE

ROWMAN AND LITTLEFIELD
Totowa, New Jersey

First published London 1893

This edition first published in the United States
1973 by Rowman and Littlefield, Totowa, New Jersey.

Reprinted 1976

Library of Congress Cataloging in Publication Data

Larminie, William, d. 1900.
  West Irish folk-tales and romances.

  Reprint of the 1893 ed.
  1. Tales, Irish. I. Title.
GR147.L3 1973   398.2'09417   72–12675
ISBN 0–87471–155–X

PRINTED IN THE UNITED STATES OF AMERICA

INTRODUCTION.

WHATEVER profit might, from the scientific point of view, be considered likely to spring from a study of Gaelic folk-lore, it would probably be considered beforehand that it would come from the study of the material as a single body, uniform throughout, and, as such, to be brought into comparison with the folk-lore of other countries. When, however, we come to an actual survey of the material, certain appearances present themselves which lead us to expect that, possibly, a large part of our gain will accrue from the observation of the differences which characterise different parts of the material within itself. Ireland, though an island of moderate extent, is yet sufficiently large to contain districts far enough apart to isolate in some degree their respective peasant populations; while it is also admitted that the homogeneity of the Gaelic tongue does not indicate a corresponding homogeneity of race. It may turn out, in fact, ultimately, that we have in Ireland, not one, but several bodies of folk-lore placed in relations most favourable for aiding in the solution of certain problems; while, finally, we shall, by a comparison with the Gaelic folk-lore of Scotland, obtain a still wider field for similar observations and inferences.

It is true, unfortunately, that our Irish material is not by any means what it might have been, either in quantity or quality; its defects being such that any conclusions arrived at through the line of investigation here to be suggested must at present be considered of a very provisional nature. Of the folk-lore of the large province of Munster we know next to nothing. I have myself hitherto been able to make no attempt at collection in the southern counties. Some of Mr. Curtin's stories were probably obtained in Kerry; but he has not told us which. We have, therefore, nothing to fall back upon but the somewhat sophisticated little fairy tales of Crofton Croker. For Leinster, we are better off, as we have the Wexford tales of Kennedy. For the inland parts of Connaught we have Dr. Hyde's volume; for the coast of Connaught and Donegal, the tales included in this book, and many others in my possession not yet published.

With regard to Crofton Croker's tales, it needs but a small acquaintance with Ireland to be assured that they are not peculiar to Munster.

The cluricaun still pursues his trade of boot-making by the shores of Achill Sound in Mayo. Donegal knows all that the south ever knew on the subject, and has perhaps even a greater wealth of information. It is admitted that in the city of Dublin the tribe does not now exist; but such is not the case even in this highly-civilised watering-place of Bray, only twelve miles distant from the metropolis. In a word, this minor mythology was, may we not say still is, common to the whole island.

The fairies, however, do not very often form the subjects of the longer detailed narratives. Let me now turn to these. Among the Connaught stories I have found a good many parallels on the coast to those of the inland districts, though I have not included any in this volume. In Donegal, on the other hand, while I have obtained only two partial variants of the inland Connaught tales, I have found several close parallels to the Connaught coast tales—a fact, however, which may be accounted for by the partially Donegalese descent of the Achill people. If we now bring the Wexford tales into comparison, it will be found that they do not contain many parallels to those of the other districts. I know of only five from Connaught, and two from the more distant Donegal, both variants of two of the Connaught tales, one of them, perhaps the best known of all such stories—no other, indeed, than Mr. Lang's "far-travelled tale"— that of "The Three Tasks"; the other, of which I obtained complete versions in Galway and in Mayo, and which I know to exist in Donegal, is represented in this volume by "Morraha Brian More," and in Kennedy by the "Fis fá an aon Sgeul." Now this latter does not appear to be much known except in Ireland; but it will hardly be contended that it was independently invented in the four Irish counties in which it has been discovered. Still less would this be maintained regarding the other. The tale, which has proved its popularity by flourishing in three quarters of the globe, shows the same quality on a smaller scale by flourishing in at least three provinces of Ireland.

And perhaps this is the best place to note that the theory of independent origin is contrary to one of the closest analogies to be observed in nature. When animals and plants of the same species are found in widely-distant regions, no naturalist assumes for a moment that they originated separately. However puzzling the problem may be, the student of nature seeks to solve it by explanations of a very different kind; and already many of the most difficult cases have yielded their secret to patient investigation. It will assuredly turn out to be the same with folk-tales. As regards Ireland we see that there is a presumption, which will scarcely be contested, in favour of the view that certain entire tales were dispersed from a common centre, thus showing on a small scale the working of the whole process. When, however, we come to parts of tales, such as special phrases, rhymes, etc., the evidence of a common origin is beyond question. There are plenty of minor examples in this volume; but here I would direct special attention to the three sea-runs which occur in "Bioultach," "King Mananaun," and "The Champion of the Red Belt," found in Galway, Mayo, and Donegal respectively (see *Note*, pp. 253-4). I think it difficult for any one who reads these and notes their likenesses and their differences, not to believe that they were originally composed by one person. The variations are easily accounted for by imperfect recollection, substitutions for forgotten phrases, and all the gradual alterations sure to arise in the case of irregular oral transmission among peasant narrators.

The evidence, then, seems so far to show that the fairy belief is common to all Ireland; that of the more elaborate traditional narratives, a certain small proportion seems to be widely diffused, while the larger portion separates into divisions peculiar to certain districts, the greatest divergence between one locality and another occurring when the localities are most widely separated.

Now, that there should be any considerable
divergence seems surprising when the facts are
fully taken into account. Ireland is not a large
country. For centuries—we do not know how
many—before the Norman invasion, the inhabitants
had spoken Gaelic. The absence of political
unity, the ceaseless wars and forays, must all
have tended to fuse the population and obliterate
original differences much more than a settled state
of society. Yet they exist. The differences in
folk-lore are not greater than other differences.
Ethnologists know that the so-called Gaelic race
is really a compound one, containing in addition
to the true Celtic (Aryan) element probably two
that are not Aryan—a Mongolian or Finnish
element, and an Iberian element. Very little
attempt has hitherto been made to settle in what
parts of the country these elements respectively
preponderate ; but that there must be some pre-
ponderance of different races in different localities
is shown clearly enough by the varying physical
types. It is beyond question that Donegal differs
from Connaught, and that both differ from
Munster ; and when we find that, in spite of a
coexistence of at least two thousand years in the
same island, and the possession of a common
language, different districts have a different folk-
lore, is it extravagant to surmise that these different
bodies are due to varying racial deposits ?

Let us now compare Ireland as a whole with the Scotch Highlands. The language of both is still, as for fifteen hundred years, practically the same. The inhabitants are of closely-allied race, in part identical, and for many centuries a constant communication was kept up between both countries. The folk-lore is partly alike, partly unlike. The similarity is occasionally very great. There are entire tales which are all but identical as told on both sides of the sea. There is identity of phrases and sentences. In Campbell's version of the "far-travelled tale," "The Battle of the Birds," occurs a striking phrase, in which the raven is said to have carried a man "over seven benns and seven glens and seven mountain moors." Nearly the same phrase occurs in Kennedy's version— "seven mountains (benns), seven glens and seven moors," which is the more surprising, as this story had passed, one does not know how long before, from its Gaelic into its English dress. Compare the phrase from "Morraha" in the present volume —"he sat down and gave a groan and the chair broke in pieces"—with Campbell's "The King of Assaroe"—"his heart was so heavy the chair broke under him." Many other examples could be given. We have before our eyes, so far as Irish and Scotch folk-lore are similar, an example of how two branches of a race originally so closely united as almost to form one, have for some hundreds of years drifted or been forced apart, the process being thus unfolded to us in the full light of history by which a body of folk-lore, originally one, has separated into divisions showing distinct characteristics, while it retains the strongest tokens of its original unity.

But it seems as if there was a large amount of folk-literature in each country which the other never possessed. To this I shall come presently, after I have first brought forward a comparison with German folk-lore. But before attempting that, it is desirable first to offer a few remarks on the style of the stories in this volume.

It will, I hope, be observed that the style is not uniform, but that it differs considerably from one story to another, and not so much in accordance with the narrator as with what he narrates. I must of course partially except the case of P. Minahan, whose individuality is stamped on everything that comes from him ; but this is not so with the other narrators. If " The Gloss Gavlen " be compared with the only other tale of M'Ginty's, " The King who had Twelve Sons," it will be seen that the style of the two is quite distinct, the first being noticeable for a certain archaic simplicity of which there is no trace in the other. Again, the style of " Bioultach " is surely quite different from that of T. Davis's other contribution, " The Story," in " Morraha," while the opening of the latter from

M'Grale is easily distinguishable from that of "The Little Girl who got the better of the Gentleman," or "Gilla of the Enchantments." Even Minahan varies with his subject, as will appear from a comparison of "The Woman who went to Hell" with "The Champion of the Red Belt." It seems from this as if some of the tales had a certain indestructibility of style, an original colour which passed unaltered through the minds of perhaps generations of reciters, this colour being determined at first by the character of the subject. In general, the tales of fierce fighting champions, of the more terrible monsters, sorcerers and the like, have a certain fierceness, if one may use the word, of style ; while those of more domestic incident are told with quietness and tenderness.

Let me now briefly compare the folk-tales of Germany with those of the Scotch Highlands.

It cannot, I think, escape notice in reading Grimm's collection, that a very large number of the tales bear a strong impress of quiet domesticity. They are very properly named "household" in more senses than one. And this is a matter not merely of style but of substance. The incidents are, to a vast extent, domestic in character. There is no occasion to give a long list of the tales I refer to. I may mention as types "The Three Spinners," which turns entirely on the results of domestic drudgery to the female figure ; and

"Thrush-Beard," a tale analogous to "The Taming of the Shrew" legend. But this domestic stamp becomes more fully apparent when we bring into contrast the Highland stories. Among these there are indeed parallels to Grimm ; but they are relatively few, and there is a whole class of incidents and stories of which little trace is found in the German collection. The domestic incident all but disappears. The tales are more romantic, picturesque, extravagant. The giants and monsters are more frequent and fearful. The stories of helping animals—and this is very characteristic—though not entirely absent, are far less numerous than in Grimm.

Now, turning to Ireland, we find that both classes of story meet upon Irish soil. Without making any allowance for the imperfect collection of our folk-lore, and the quantity that must have been lost owing to the lateness of our attempts to rescue it, it must be admitted that we have the domestic story fairly well developed. The two tales from Grimm that I have named, as well as many others, have the closest possible parallels in Kennedy, and I have myself met with additional examples on the coast of Connaught. The romantic and extravagant class of tales which flourish in the Highlands have also good representatives in our oral literature. Some specimens may be read in this volume. In one story, " Gilla of the Enchantments," is found a striking combination of the two. The story is, in part, a close variant of Kennedy's " Twelve Wild Geese," but it also contains, in addition to other matter, the wild incident of the daily cutting off of the brothers' heads by the sister, which is equally wanting in the variant to be found in Grimm.

The question now arises, How are these contrasts and similarities to be accounted for ? Must we suppose them to be due to mere accident ? If not, what law has been at work? Why have different kinds of tales drifted in different directions? What current of distribution has carried one set of tales to Scotland, part of the same and part of a different set to Ireland, while Germany has received a much larger share of the latter than Ireland, though in the other she has been left poor ? It is clearly not commercial intercourse that has been at work, nor exogamy, nor slavery. Some other agency has to be sought for.

In the case of ancient Greece we have an instance in which an exceptionally rich body of legend has been proved to consist of elements brought from divers nations and races. The birthplace of many of the most considerable personages in Greek mythology has been found in Asian lands. The Centaurs, Perseus, Dionysus and Semele, Artemis, Adonis and Aphrodite herself, are believed to be all Asiatic in origin. Nay,

more.   These Orientals are shown to belong to
two distinct races commingled in Babylonia : the
Semites, who may have had distant affinities with
the Iberians of the West ; and the Accadians, whose
connections were Mongol.   It is true that the
Greeks are held to have received these additions
to their own store by means of commercial intercourse.   The Phœnicians, those restless honey-
gatherers of the old Mediterranean world, went
about everywhere fertilising Western flowers with
Eastern pollen ; but in the case of the wild and
barbarous north-west a similar agency cannot be
found ; and while we are justified in taking the
hint supplied by the discovery of the compound
racial nature of Greek myth, we are compelled by
circumstances to seek for a different solution of
the problem.

I have already adverted to the differences of
race which exist in Ireland, more or less masked
by the long predominance of the Aryan Gael.
Such differences are not confined to Ireland.   It
is now admitted that the apparent predominance
of the Aryan over most of Europe is, to a great
extent, one of language merely.   Furthermore,
the elements which make up our population are
found everywhere ; the differences, mental and
physical, which characterise different nations,
being mainly due, first, to the minor variations
which mark the branches of the great stocks, such

as Celt, Teuton, and Slav among the Aryans, and secondly, to the continually varying proportions in which the different elements are blended. The principal fact is, that far the larger part of the Old World, excluding Africa, is occupied by three or four varieties of man, such as the Aryan, the Mongol, and the Iberian ; the others, even when as important as the Semitic, holding very limited areas, and subject to continual contact with those more predominant. Of these again, it is worthy of remark that the most widely spread is not the Aryan, but the Mongol. The latter, in addition to the vast regions which are his openly, such as Japan, China, Central Asia, and his outlying posts in Europe, Finland, Hungary, and Turkey, is recognised by the type as leading a masked existence in the most western portions of our quarter of the globe. "Scratch the Russian and you will find the Tartar" is a saying which may be applied, *mutatis mutandis*, to many a nation much more remote from Central Asia ; nor can we be surprised that such should be the case when we call to mind that this powerful branch of mankind has actually, within recent historical times, run the Aryan a neck-and-neck race for outward supremacy, while to the Semites he has scarcely left even their deserts.

With regard to the Iberian race, it has only to be noted that its distribution in the south and west of Europe is very extensive. It is still almost

b

wholly predominant in Spain and Portugal. It probably constituted in old times, as now, the main non-Aryan element in Mediterranean Europe. North-westward it has had a wide extension into France, Britain, and Ireland, and probably into Scandinavia and other countries; while it is not impossible that to it also belong in part the non-Aryan inhabitants of Hindustan.

Applying these facts to Germany, the Scotch Highlands, and Ireland, do we not obtain a hint as to the phenomenon of folk-lore distribution? One race, let us say mainly Aryan, in Germany; another race, much less Aryan, in the Scotch Highlands; a third, a more even blend of the two —of Aryan and non-Aryan—in Ireland.

This theory seems to me to be only such a modification of a theory which originally prevailed as is now required by the facts. It was at first believed, apparently is still believed by some, that all these tales originally belonged to the Aryans alone. As soon, however, as it was found that many of them were the possession of races far removed from Aryan contact, it was at once seen that a modification of view was imperative. Then came the independent origin theory; and, amongst others of later birth, one which has recently attracted much attention—the Indian theory. This seems to me to involve the truth of several propositions which are surely a little hard to accept. We must hold, first, that the Aryans, when they entered India, had no folk-tales, because, according to the hypothesis, they carried none elsewhere; next, that the tales were either invented by the Aryans after they entered India, or were learned by them from the earlier peoples of that country. But that tales of one country, or one race, should have had a peculiar ability to diffuse themselves, wanting to all others, is a proposition that tries one's faith. Reverting again to the analogy already used, we know that there are animals common to India and Ireland whose original home was in neither country. There are men of the same Aryan descent by the Shannon and by the Indus whose ancestors had not their first common habitation by either river. And the folk-tales, so far as they are Aryan, did not originate south of the Himalayas, or west of the Irish Sea. But they cannot all be Aryan. Nothing could antecedently be more improbable than the suggestion that they were; and we might fairly regard it as refuted even if we had nothing to go on but the literary character of the tales. They bear the stamp of the genius of more than one race. The pure and placid but often cold imagination of the Aryan has been at work on some. In others we trace the more picturesque fancy, the fierceness and sensuality, the greater sense of artistic elegance belonging to races whom the Aryan, in spite of his occasional faults of hardness and coarseness, has, on the whole, left behind him. But as the greatest results in the realm of the highest art have always been achieved in the case of certain blends of Aryan with other blood, I should hardly deem it extravagant if it were asserted that in the humbler regions of the folk-tale we might trace the working of the same law. The process which has gone on may in part have been as follows :—Every race which has acquired very definite characteristics must have been for a long time isolated. The Aryans, during their period of isolation, probably developed many of their folk-germs into their larger myths, owing to the greater constructiveness of their imagination, and thus, in a way, they used up part of their material. Afterwards, when they became blended with other races less advanced, they acquired fresh material to work on. We have in Ireland an instance to hand, of which a brief discussion may help to illustrate the whole race theory.

The larger Irish legendary literature divides itself into three cycles—the divine, the heroic, the Fenian. Of these three the last is so well known orally in Scotland that it has been a matter of dispute to which country it really belongs. It belongs, in fact, to both. Here, however, comes in a strange contrast with the other cycles. The first is, so far as I am aware, wholly unknown in

Scotland, the second comparatively unknown. What is the explanation ? Professor Zimmer not having established his late-historical view as regards Fionn, and the general opinion among scholars having tended of recent years towards the mythical view, we want to know why there is so much more community in one case than in the other. Mr. O'Grady long since seeing this difficulty, and then believing Fionn to be historical, was induced to place the latter in point of time before Cuchullin and his compeers. But this view is, of course, inadmissible when Fionn is seen not to be historical at all. There remains but one explanation. The various bodies of legend in question are, so far as Ireland is concerned, only earlier or later as they came into the island with the various races to which they belonged. The wider prevalence, then, of the Fionn Saga would indicate that it belonged to an early race occupying both Ireland and Scotland. Then entered the Aryan Gael, and for him, henceforth, as the ruler of the island, his own gods and heroes were sung by his own bards. His legends became the subject of what I may call the court poetry, the aristocratic literature. When he conquered Scotland, he took with him his own gods and heroes ; but in the latter country the bardic system never became established, and hence we find but feeble echoes of the heroic cycle among the mountains of the North. That this is the explanation is shown by what took place in Ireland. Here the heroic cycle has been handed down in remembrance almost solely by the bardic literature. The popular memory retains but few traces of it. Its essentially aristocratic character is shown by the fact that the people have all but forgotten it if they ever knew it. But the Fenian cycle has not been forgotten. Prevailing everywhere, still cherished by the conquered peoples, it held its ground in Scotland and Ireland alike, forcing its way in the latter country even into the written literature, and so securing a twofold lease of existence. That it did not deserve this wider popularity is evident enough. Interesting though it be, it is not equal in interest to the heroic cycle. The tales of the latter, though fewer in number, less bulky in amount, have upon them the impress of the larger constructive sweep of the Aryan imagination. Their characters are nobler; the events are more significant. They form a much more closely compacted epic whole. The Fenian tales, in some respects more picturesque, are less organised. It would be difficult to construct out of them a coherent epic plot; and what is, perhaps, not the least in significance, they have far more numerous, more extended, more intimate connections with the folk-tale.

The Fenian cycle, in a word, is non-Aryan folk-

literature partially subjected to Aryan treatment.
It occupies accordingly a middle position. Above
the rank of the folk-tale it has been elevated;
but to the dignity of the heroic legend 'it has not
attained.

The tales included in the present volume form
part of a large collection, which I began to make as
far back as the year 1884. All have been taken
down in the same way—that is to say, word for
word from the dictation of the peasant narrators,
all by myself, with the exception of two taken
down by Mr. Lecky in precisely similar fashion;
difficult and doubtful parts being gone over again
and again. Sometimes the narrators can explain
difficulties. Sometimes other natives of the place
can help you. But after every resource of this
kind has been exhausted, a certain number of
doubtful words and phrases remain, with regard
to which—well, one can only do one's best.

The districts from which the tales were obtained
are three in number, each represented by two
narrators. Renvyle, the most southern of the
three, is situated in Connemara. It is a narrow
peninsula, forming the extreme north-western
point of the county of Galway, jutting out opposite Mayo. Terence Davis is a labourer pure
and simple, a man of about forty-five years of
age, and blind of one eye. Some of his tales

he got from his mother. Michael Faherty was, when I first made his acquaintance, a lad of about seventeen. He was recommended, as the best pupil in the National School, to Mr. Lecky, who, finding him intelligent, selected him as the best person from whom, on account of his youth, the very latest development of the language could be learnt. He lived with his uncle, who had, or has still, a small holding on the Blake property, and who was also a pilot and repairer of boats. Both his tales were taken down by Mr. Lecky. Next in order, going northward, comes Achill Island, distant some twenty-five miles from Renvyle by sea, more than sixty miles by land.* Two narrators from that locality are also represented in the book. One of them, Pat. M‘Grale, is a man of middle age, a cottier with a small holding, and besides, a Jack-of-all-trades, something of a boatman and fisherman, " a botch of a tailor," to use his own words, and ready for any odd job. He can read Irish, but had very little literature on which to exercise his accomplishment. He knows some long poems by heart, and is possessed of various odds and ends of learning, accurate and not. John M‘Ginty, a man of Donegal descent and name, has also some land ; but his holding is so small that he is to a great extent a labourer for others, and was engaged on relief works when I

* The Sound, very narrow, is now bridged over.

first came to know him. He, also, is a middle-aged man. He knows many Ossianic poems by heart, which, he told me, his father taught him, verse by verse.

Glencolumkill is the extreme south-west corner of Donegal, remote, like Achill and Renvyle. It is chiefly represented by the tales of Pat. Minahan, from whom I obtained more stories than from any other one man. He said he was eighty years of age ; but he was in full possession of all his faculties. He also had a holding on which he still worked industriously. He had no children ; but his nephew, who lived with him, made up for all deficiencies of that nature. His style, with its short, abrupt sentences, is always remarkable, and at its best I think excellent. Jack Gillespie, known as Jack-Anne—the latter his mother's name —to distinguish him from other Jack Gillespies, was a man of sixty or over, also a cottier.

The tales were written down in places sufficiently varied ;—from the Renvyle library to the neat little farmhouse parlour at Malinmore, where I spent so many a winter's evening, solitary but for the occasional visits of some one or other of my story-tellers ;—from little smoky cabins, with inquisitive hens hopping on the table, to the unroofed freedom of rock or brae, under summer skies, by those thrice-lovely shores of Renvyle ; by the scarcely less beautiful, though far more rugged, crags and cliffs of Achill ; by "the wild sea-banks" of what has been described as the "grandest coast in Europe" —that of Glencolumkill.

The beauty of Scotch scenery has been discovered by one critic to be reflected in the picturesqueness of the Scotch tales. I am not without hope that a like influence has contributed something of a like quality to those now submitted to the reader.

WILLIAM LARMINIE.

CONTENTS.

THE GLOSS GAVLEN.

Narrator, JOHN MCGINTY, *Valley, Achill Island,*
co Mayo.

THE Gobaun Seer and his son went eastward
to the eastern world to Balar Beimann to
make for him a palace. "Shorten the road, my
son," said the father. The son ran out before him
on the road, and the father returned home on that
day. The second day they went travelling, and
the father told his son to shorten the road. He
ran out in front of his father the second day, and
the father returned home.

"What's the cause of your returning home like
that?" said the wife of the young Gobaun.

"My father asks me to shorten the road. I
run out on the road before him, and he returns."

"Do you begin to-morrow at a story he has
never heard, and I'll go bail he will not return.
And do you never be in any place that the women
are not on your side."

They went travelling the third day, and the

young Gobaun began at a story his father never heard, and he returned no more till they came to the eastern world. Then they made the palace for Balar Beimann, and he did not wish to let them go back, for fear they should make for another man a palace as good as his.

" Take away the scaffolding" (said he); for he wanted to let them die on the top of the building. Balar Beimann had a girl, who went by under the building in the morning.

" Young Gobaun," said she, " go on thy wisdom. I think it is easier to throw seven stones down than to put one up as far as you."

" That's true for you," said young Gobaun.

They began to let down the work. When Balar Beimann heard that they were throwing down the works, he ordered back the scaffolding till they were down on the ground.

"Now," said the old Gobaun Seer, " there is a crookedness in your work, and if I had three tools I left after me at home, I would straighten the work, and there would not be any work in the world to compare with it. The names of the tools are—Crooked against Crooked, Corner against Corner, and Engine against deceit;* and there is not a man to get them but your own son. You will find," said he, " a woman with one hand,

* Or, perhaps, " trick against treachery."

and a child with one eye, in the house, and a stack of corn at the door."

The father then gave him a ship and sent him over to Erin. He was travelling ever till he found out the house ; and he went into it. He asked if that was the house of young Gobaun. The woman said it was.

" He said to me there was a woman with one hand, and a child with one eye in the house, and a stack of corn at the door."

"Don't you see," said she, "that I have only one hand, and don't you see this stick in the hand of the child ? I don't know what moment he won't put it in his eye and take the eye out of himself; and don't you see the stack of corn outside at the door ? "

He asked then for the three tools.

" What three tools ? " said she.

" They are Corner against Corner, Crooked against Crooked, and Engine against deceit."

She understood then that they (*i.e.* her husband and his father) would never come home, if she did not understand these words.

"The three tools that are called Crooked against Crooked, Corner against Corner, and Engine against deceit, they are down in this chest."

She went then and opened the chest, and told him to stoop down to the bottom, that she was not tall enough. He stooped, and when she got him bent down, she threw him into the chest and closed it, and told him he should stay there till young Gobaun and old Gobaun came home and their pay for their service with them.

She sent word to Balar Beimann that she had his son in confinement, till young Gobaun and old Gobaun came home. He gave them a ship and sent them home with their pay; and she let Balar Beimann's son back to him again. When they were going home, Balar asked Gobaun what smith would he get to put irons on his palace.

"There is no smith in Erin better than Gavid-jeen Go."

When the old Gobaun came home he told Gavidjeen Go to take no pay from him for putting the irons on his palace, except the Gloss:

"If twenty barrels were put under her, she would fill the twenty barrels."

Balar Beimann then wrote to the Gavidjeen Go that he would give him the Gloss if he would make irons for his palace. But when he sent the Gloss, he did not give the byre-rope, and he knew that when he did not give that, she would go from him.

This is the bargain that Gavidjeen Go made then with every champion that came to him :—to mind the cow and bring her safe home to him at evening; he would make a sword for every champion who would mind her. She would pas-

ture in the daytime at Cruahawn, of Connaught,
and drink at Loch Ayachir-a-Guigalu, in Ulster,
in the evening.

Kian, the son of Contje, came to him to have
a sword made. He told him he would make it,
but that the bargain would be to mind the Gloss
that day.

" If she is not home with you to me in the evening, you must lay down your head on the anvil,
that I may cut it off with your own sword."

Kian, the son of Contje, went then and took
hold of her by the tail. When he came home in
the evening, " Here is the Gloss outside," said he
to Gavidjeen Go. There was a champion inside
in the forge, whose name was the Laughing
Knight. He ran out and said to Kian :

" The smith is about to put tempering on your
sword, and unless you have hold of it, there will
be no power in it when you wield it."

When Kian, the son of Contje, went in, he
forgot to drive in the Gloss. Gavidjeen Go
asked him, " Where is the Gloss ? "

" There she is, outside the door."

" Put her in," said he.

When he went out she was gone.

" Lay down your head upon the anvil, that I
may cut it off you."

" I am asking of you the favour of three days,
to go and seek her."

"I will give you that," said he.

He went with himself then, and was following her tracks till he came to the sea. He was up and down on the shore, plucking his hair from his head, in trouble after the Gloss. There was a man out on the sea in a currach. He rowed in to him. It was the tawny Mananaun, the son of Lir. He asked him—

"What is the matter with you to-day?"

He told him.

"How much will you give to any one who will leave you in the place where the Gloss is?"

"I have nothing to give him."

"I will ask nothing of you, but the half of all you gain till you come back."

"I will give you that," said Kian, son of Contje.

"Be into the currach."

In the winking of an eye he left him over in the kingdoms of the cold; nor on that island was a morsel cooked ever, but they ate every kind of food raw. Kian, son of Contje, made a fire, and began to cook his food. When Balar Beimann heard the like was there, he took him to be his cook, his story-teller, and his fireman. Well, Balar Beimann had one daughter, and a prediction was made that she would have a son, who would kill his grandfather. He then put her into prison for fear a man would come near her; and it was he himself who would go to her with food, and the companion with her was a dummy woman. Mananaun left this enchantment with Kian, son of Contje, that any lock he laid his hand on would open and shut after him. He was looking at Balar Beimann going to this house, to his daughter, with food for her, and he went himself after him to the house, and he laid his hand on the lock and opened the door, and found none but the two women there. He made a fire for them. He was coming there ever, till a child happened to her. He was then going to depart, when the boy was born. He went to the king and told him he must depart.

" Why are you going ? " said he.

" It is because accidents have happened to me since I came into this island. I must go."

" What is the accident ? " said he.

" A child has happened to me."

Balar had two sons on another island learning druidism. They came home to the palace to their father.

" Father," said a man of them, " your story-teller, your cook, and your fireman will give you your sufficiency of trouble."

Kian, son of Contje, was listening to them speaking. He went to the daughter of Balar Beimann, and told her what her brother said.

" Well," said she, " it is now time for you to

be going. That is the byre-rope of the Gloss, hanging on the wall. She will be as quick as you; and take with you the boy."

He went then till he came to the place where Mananaun put him out. Mananaun told him, when he was in difficulty, to think of him and he would come. He now came on the instant.

"Be in the currach," said Mananaun, "and make haste, or Balar Beimann will drown us, if he can. But greater is my druidism than his," said the tawny Mananaun, the son of Lir.

He jumped into the currach, and the Gloss jumped in as soon as he. Balar Beimann followed them, and raised the sea in a storm before them and behind them, nor did Mananaun aught but stretch out his hand and make the sea calm. Balar then set fire to the sea before them in hopes of burning them, but Mananaun threw out a stone, and extinguished the sea.

"Now, Kian, son of Contje, you are safe and sound home, and what will you give me for it ? "

"I have nothing but the boy, and we will not go to make two halves of him, but I will give him to you entirely."

"I am thankful to you. That is what I was wanting. There will be no champion in the world as good as he," said Mananaun.

This is the name that Mananaun baptized him with—the Dul Dauna. He brought him up with feats of activity and championship. He and Mananaun were out one day on the sea, and they saw the fleet of Balar Beimann sailing. The Dul Dauna put a ring to his eye, and he saw his grandfather on the deck walking, but he did not know it was his grandfather. He (took) a dart from his pocket and flung it at him and killed him. The prophecy was then fulfilled.

MORRAHA,

*BRIAN MORE, SON OF THE HIGH-KING OF ERIN FROM
THE WELL OF ENCHANTMENTS OF BINN EDIN*

Narrator, P. McGrale, *Dugort, Achill Island, co. Mayo.*

MORRAHA rose in the morning and washed his hands and face, and said his prayers, and ate his food ; and he asked God to prosper the day for him ; and he went down to the brink of the sea, and he saw a currach, short and green, coming towards him ; and in it there was but one youthful champion, and he playing hurly from prow to stern of the currach. He had a hurl of gold and a ball of silver ; and he stopped not till the currach was in on the shore ; and he drew her up on the green grass, and put fastening on her for a day and a year, whether he should be there all that time or should only be on land for an hour by the clock. And Morraha saluted the young man in words intelligent, intelligible, such as (were spoken) at that time ; and the other saluted him in the same fashion, and asked him

would he play a game of cards with him; and
Morraha said that he had not the wherewithal;
and the other answered that he was never without
a candle or the making of it ; and he put his hand
in his pocket and drew out a table and two chairs
and a pack of cards, and they sat down on the
chairs and went to the card-playing. The first
game Morraha won, and the slender red champion
bade him make his claim ; and he said that
the land above him should be filled with stock
of sheep in the morning. It was well; and he
played no second game, but home he went.

The next day Morraha went to the brink of
the sea, and the young man came in the currach
and asked him would he play cards ; and they
played ; and Morraha won. And the young man
bade him make his claim ; and he said that the
land above should be filled with cattle in the
morning. It was well; and he played no other
game, but went home.

And on the third morning Morraha went to
the brink of the sea, and he saw the young man
coming. And he drew up his boat on the shore
and asked him would he play cards. And they
played, and Morraha won the game ; and the
young man bade him give his claim. And he
said he should have a castle and of women the
finest and the fairest ; and they were his. It
was well ; and the young man went away.

On the fourth day the woman asked him how he had found himself, and he told her. "And I am going out" (said he) "to play again to-day."

"I cross" (forbid) "you to go again to him. If you have won so much, you will lose more; and have no more to do with him."

But he went against her will, and he saw the currach coming; and the young man was driving his balls from end to end of the currach; he had balls of silver and a hurl of gold, and he stopped not till he drew his boat on the shore, and made her fast for a year and a day. And Morraha and he saluted each other; and he asked Morraha if he would play a game of cards, and they played, and he won. And Morraha said to him, "Give your claim now."

Said he, "You will hear it too soon. I lay on you the bonds of the art of the druid, not to sleep two nights in one house, nor finish a second meal at the one table, till you bring me the sword of light and news of the death of Anshgayliacht."

He went home to his wife and sat down in a chair, and gave a groan, and the chair broke in pieces.

"It is the son of a king under spells you are," said his wife; "and you had better have taken my counsel than that the spells should be on you."

He said to her to bring news of the death of Anshgayliacht and the sword of light to the slender red champion.

"Go out," said she, "in the morning of the morrow, and take the bridle in the window, and shake it; and whatever beast, handsome or ugly, puts the head in it, take that one with you. Do not speak a word to her till she speaks to you; and take with you three pint bottles of ale and three sixpenny loaves, and do the thing she tells you; and when she runs to my father's land, on a height above the court, she will shake herself, and the bells will ring, and my father will say Brown Allree is in the land. And if the son of a king or queen is there, bring him to me on your shoulders; but if it is the son of a poor man, let him come no further."

He rose in the morning, and took the bridle that was in the window, and went out and shook it; and Brown Allree came and put her head in it. And he took the three loaves and three bottles of ale, and went riding; and when he was riding she bent her head down to take hold of her feet with her mouth, in hopes he would speak in ignorance; but he spoke not a word during the time, and the mare at last spoke to him, and said to him to dismount and give her her dinner. He gave her the sixpenny loaf toasted, and a bottle of ale to drink. "Sit up

now riding, and take good heed of yourself:
there are three miles of fire I have to clear at a
leap."

She cleared the three miles of fire at a leap,
and asked if he were riding, and he said he was.
They went on then, and she told him to dismount
and give her a meal; and he did so, and gave
her a sixpenny loaf and a bottle ; and she consumed them, and said to him there were before
them three miles of hill covered with steel thistles,
and that she must clear it.   And she cleared the
hill with a leap, and she asked him if he were
still riding, and he said he was.   They went on,
and she went not far before she told him to give
her a meal, and he gave her the bread and the
bottleful.   And she went over three miles of sea
with a leap, and she came then to the land of
the King of France ; and she went up on a height
above the castle, and she shook herself and neighed,
and the bells rang ; and the king said that it was
Brown Allree was in the land.   "Go out," said
he, "and if it is the son of a king or queen, carry
him in on your shoulders ; if it is not, leave him
there."

They went out ; and the stars of the son of a
king were on his breast ; and they lifted him high
on their shoulders and bore him in to the king.
And they passed the night cheerfully, with playing   and   with   drinking,   with   sport   and   with

diversion, till the whiteness of the day came upon the morrow morning.

Then the young king told the cause of his journey, and he asked of the queen her counsel and consent, and to give him counsel and good luck, and the woman told him everything she advised him to do. " Go now," said she, " and take with you the best mare in the stable, and go to the door of Rough Niall of the speckled rock, and knock, and call on him to give you news of the death of Anshgayliacht and the sword of light ; and let the horse's back be to the door, and apply the spurs, and away with you."

And in the morning he did so, and he took the best horse from the stable and rode to the door of Niall, and turned the horse's back to the door, and demanded news of the death of Anshgayliacht and the sword of light ; and he applied the spurs, and away with him. And Niall followed him, and, as he was passing the gate, cut the horse in two. And the mother was there with a dish of puddings and flesh, and she threw it in his eyes and blinded him, and said, " Fool, whatever kind of man it is that's mocking you, isn't that a fine condition you have got on your father's horse ? "

On the morning of the next day, Morraha rose, and took another horse from the stable, and went again to the door of Niall, and knocked and demanded news of the death of Anshgayliacht and the sword of light, and applied the spurs to the horse and away with him. And Niall followed, and as he was passing the gate, cut the horse in two and took half the saddle with him; and his mother met him and threw the flesh in his eyes and blinded him.

And on the third day, Morraha went also to the door of Niall; and Niall followed him, and as he was passing the gate, cut away the saddle from under him and the clothes from his back. Then his mother said to Niall,—

"Whatever fool it is that's mocking you, he is out yonder in the little currach, going home; and take good heed to yourself, and don't sleep one wink for three days."

And for three days the little currach was there before him, and then his mother came to him and said,—

"Sleep as much as you want now. He is gone."

And he went to sleep, and there was heavy sleep on him, and Morraha went in and took hold of the sword that was on the bed at his head. And the sword thought to draw itself out of the hand of Morraha; but it failed. And then it gave a cry, and it wakened Niall, and Niall said it was a rude and rough thing to come into his house like that; and said Morraha to him,—

" Leave your much talking, or I will cut the head off you. Tell me the news of the death of Anshgayliacht."

" Oh, you can have my head."

" But your head is no good to me ; tell me the story."

" Oh," said Niall's wife, " you must get the story."

" Oh " [said Morraha], " is the woman your wife ? "

" Oh," said the man, " it is not you who have the story."

" Oh," said she, " you will tell it to us."

" Well," said the man, "let us sit down together till I tell the story. I thought no one would ever get it ; but now it will be heard by all."

THE STORY.

(*The Story is from the narrative of* TERENCE DAVIS, *of Renvyle, co. Galway.*)

When I was growing up, my mother taught me the language of the birds ; and when I got married, I used to be listening to their conversation ; and I would be laughing; and my wife would be asking me what was the reason of my laughing, but I did not like to tell her, as women are always asking questions. We went out walking one fine morning, and the birds were arguing with one another. One of them said to another,—

" Why should you be making comparison with me, when there is not a king nor knight that does not come to look at my tree ? "

" Oh, what advantage has your tree over mine, on which there are three rods of magic and mastery growing ? "

When I heard them arguing, and knew that the rods were there, I began to laugh.

"Oh," asked my wife, " why are you always laughing ? I believe it is at myself you are jesting, and I'll walk with you no more."

"Oh, it is not about you I am laughing. It is because I understand the language of the birds."

Then I had to tell her what the birds were saying to one another ; and she was greatly delighted, and she asked me to go home, and she gave orders to the cook to have breakfast ready at six o'clock in the morning. I did not know why she was going out early, and breakfast was ready in the morning at the hour she appointed. She asked me to go out walking. I went with her. She went to the tree, and asked me to cut a rod for her.

"Oh, I will not cut it. Are we not better without it ? "

" I will not leave this until I get the rod, to see if there is any good in it."

I cut the rod and gave it to her. She turned

from me and struck a blow on a stone, and
changed it; and she struck a second blow on
me, and made of me a black raven, and she
went home and left me after her. I thought she
would come back; she did not come, and I had
to go into a tree till morning. In the morning,
at six o'clock, there was a bellman out, proclaim-
ing that every one who killed a raven would
get a fourpenny bit. At last you would not find
man or boy without a gun, nor, if you were to
walk three miles, a raven that was not killed. I
had to make a nest in the top of the parlour
chimney, and hide myself all day till night came,
and go out to pick up a bit to support me, till
I spent a month. Here she is herself (to say)
if it is a lie I am telling.

"It is not," said she.

Then I saw her out walking. I went up to
her, and I thought she would turn me back to
my own shape, and she struck me with the rod
and made of me an old white horse, and she
ordered me to be put to a cart with a man, to
draw stones from morning till night. I was
worse off then. She spread abroad a report that
I had died suddenly in my bed, and prepared a
coffin, and waked and buried me. Then she had
no trouble. But when I got tired I began to kill
every one who came near me, and I used to go
into the haggard every night and destroy the

stacks of corn ; and when a man came near me in the morning I would follow him till I broke his bones. Every one got afraid of me. When she saw I was doing mischief she came to meet me, and I thought she would change me. And she did change me, and made a fox of me. When I saw she was doing me every sort of damage I went away from her. I knew there was a badger's hole in the garden, and I went there till night came, and I made great slaughter among the geese and ducks. There she is herself to say if I am telling a lie.

"Oh! you are telling nothing but the truth, only less than the truth."

When she had enough of my killing the fowl she came out into the garden, for she knew I was in the badger's hole. She came to me and made me a wolf. I had to be off, and go to an island, where no one at all would see me, and now and then I used to be killing sheep, for there were not many of them, and I was afraid of being seen and hunted ; and so I passed a year, till a shepherd saw me among the sheep, and a pursuit was made after me. And when the dogs came near me there was no place for me to escape to from them ; but I recognised the sign of the king among the men, and I made for him, and the king cried out to stop the hounds. I took a leap upon the front of the king's saddle, and

the woman behind cried out, " My king and my
lord, kill him, or he will kill you!"

"Oh! he will not kill me. He knew me;
he must be pardoned."

And the king took me home with him, and
gave orders I should be well cared for. I was
so wise, when I got food, I would not eat one
morsel until I got a knife and fork. The man
told the king, and the king came to see if it was
true, and I got a knife and fork, and I took the
knife in one paw and the fork in the other, and
I bowed to the king. The king gave orders to
bring him drink, and it came; and the king
filled a glass of wine and gave it to me.

I took hold of it in my paw and drank it, and
thanked the king.

" Oh, on my honour, it is some king or other
has lost him, when he came on the island; and I
will keep him, as he is trained; and perhaps he
will serve us yet."

And this is the sort of king he was,—a king who
had not a child living. Eight sons were born to
him and three daughters, and they were stolen the
same night they were born. No matter what
guard was placed over them, the child would be
gone in the morning. The queen now
carrying the twelfth child, and when she was
lying in the king took me with him to watch the
baby. The women were not satisfied with me.

"Oh," said the king, "what was all your watching ever? One that was born to me I have not; and I will leave this one in the dog's care, and he will not let it go."

A coupling was put between me and the cradle, and when every one went to sleep I was watching till the person woke who attended in the daytime; but I was there only two nights, when it was near the day, I saw the hand coming down through the chimney, and the hand was so big that it took round the child altogether, and thought to take him away. I caught hold of the hand above the wrist, and as I was fastened to the cradle, I did not let go my hold till I cut the hand from the wrist, and there was a howl from the person without. I laid the hand in the cradle with the child, and as I was tired I fell asleep; and when I awoke, I had neither child nor hand; and I began to howl, and the king heard me, and he cried out that something was wrong with me, and he sent servants to see what was the matter with me, and when the messenger came, he saw me covered with blood, and he could not see the child; and he went to the king and told him the child was not to be got. The king came and saw the cradle coloured with the blood, and he cried out "where was the child gone?" and every one said it was the dog had eaten it.

The king said: "It is not: loose him, and he will get the pursuit himself."

When I was loosed, I found the scent of the blood till I came to a door of the room in which the child was. I went to the king and took hold of him, and went back again and began to tear at the door. The king followed me and asked for the key. The servant said it was in the room of the stranger woman. The king caused search to be made for her, and she was not to be found. "I will break the door," said the king, "as I can't get the key." The king broke the door, and I went in, and went to the trunk, and the king asked for a key to unlock it. He got no key, and he broke the lock. When he opened the trunk, the child and the hand were stretched side by side, and the child was asleep. The king took the hand and ordered a woman to come for the child, and he showed the hand to every one in the house. But the stranger woman was gone, and she did not see the king; and here she is herself (to say) if I am telling lies of her.

"Oh, it's nothing but the truth you have!"

The king did not allow me to be tied any more. He said there was nothing so much to wonder at as that I cut the hand off, and I tied.

The child was growing till he was a year old. And he was beginning to walk, and there was no one caring for him more than I was. He was growing till he was three, and he was running out every minute ; so the king ordered a silver chain to be put between me and the child, so that he might not go away from me. I was out with him in the garden every day, and the king was as proud as the world of the child. He would be watching him every place we went, till the child grew so wise that he would loose the chain and get off. But one day that he loosed it I failed to find him ; and I ran into the house and searched the house, but there was no getting him for me. The king cried to go out and find the child, that he had got loose from the dog. They went searching for him, but they could not find him. When they failed altogether to find him, there remained no more favour with the king towards me, and every one disliked me, and I grew weak, for I did not get a morsel to eat half the time. When summer came, I said I would try and go home to my own country. I went away one fine morning, and I went swimming, and God helped me till I came home. I went into the garden, for I knew there was a place in the garden where I could hide myself, for fear she should see me. In the morning I saw my wife out walking, and my child with her, held by the hand. I pushed out to see the child, and as he was looking about him everywhere, he saw me and called out, " I see my shaggy papa. Oh!"

said he ; "oh, my heart's love, my shaggy papa,
come here till I see you!"

I was afraid the woman would see me, as she
was asking the child where he saw me, and he
said I was up in a tree ; and the more the child
called me, the more I hid myself. The woman
took the child home with her, but I knew he
would be up early in the morning.

I went to the parlour window, and the child
was within, and he playing. When he saw me
he cried out, "Oh! my heart's love, come here
till I see you, shaggy papa." I broke the window
and went in, and he began to kiss me. I saw
the rod in front of the chimney, and I jumped
up at the rod and knocked it down. "Oh! my
heart's love, no one would give me the pretty
rod." I thought he would strike me with the
rod, but he did not. When I saw the time was
short I raised my paw, and I gave him a scratch
below the knee. "Oh! you naughty, dirty,
shaggy papa, you have hurt me so much, I'll give
yourself a blow of the rod." He struck me a
light blow, and as there was no one sin on him,
I came back to my own shape again. When he
saw a man standing before him he gave a cry,
and I took him up in my arms. The servants
heard the child. A maid came in to see what
was the matter with him. When she saw me she
gave a cry out of her, and she said, "Oh, my

soul to God, if the master isn't come to life again !"

Another came in, and said it was he really. And when the mistress heard of it, she came to see with her own eyes, for she would not believe I was there ; and when she saw me she said she'd drown herself. And I said to her, "If you yourself will keep the secret, no living man will ever get the story from me until I lose my head."

Many's the man has come asking for the story, and I never let one return ; but now every one will know it, but she is as much to blame as I. I gave you my head on the spot, and a thousand welcomes, and she cannot say I have been telling anything but the truth.

" Oh ! surely ; nor are you now."

When I saw I was in a man's shape, I said I would take the child back to his father and mother, as I knew the grief they were in after him. I got a ship, and took the child with me ; and when I was journeying I came to land on an island, and I saw not a living soul on it, only a court dark and gloomy. I went in to see was there any one in it. There was no one but an old hag, tall and frightful, and she asked me, " What sort of person are you? " I heard some one groaning in another room, and I said I was a doctor, and I asked her what ailed the person who was groaning.

"Oh," said she, "it is my son, whose hand has been bitten from his wrist by a dog."

I knew then it was the boy who was taking the child from me, and I said I would cure him if I got a good reward.

"I have nothing; but there are eight young lads and three young women, as handsome as any one ever laid eyes on, and if you cure him I will give you them."

"But tell me in what place his hand was cut from him?"

"Oh, it was out in another country, twelve years ago."

"Show me the way, that I may see him."

She brought me into a room, so that I saw him, and his arm was swelled up to the shoulder. He asked if I would cure him; and I said I would cure him if he would give me the reward his mother promised.

"Oh, I will give it; but cure me."

"Well, bring them out to me."

The hag brought them out of the room. I said I should burn the flesh that was on his arm. When I looked on him he was howling with pain. I said that I would not leave him in pain long. The thief had only one eye in his forehead. I took a bar of iron, and put it in the fire till it was red, and I said to the hag, "He will be howling at first, but will fall asleep presently, and do not wake him till he has slept as much as he wants. I will close the door when I am going out." I took the bar with me, and I stood over him, and I turned it across through his eye as far as I could. He began to bellow, and tried to catch me, but I was out and away, having closed the door. The hag asked me, " Why is he bellowing ? "

" Oh, he will be quiet presently, and will sleep for a good while, and I'll come again to have a look at him ; but bring me out the young men and the young women."

I took them with me, and I said to her, " Tell me where you got them."

" Oh, my son brought them with him, and they are all the offspring of the one king."

I was well satisfied, and I had no liking for delay to get myself free from the hag, and I took them on board the ship, and the child I had myself. I thought the king might leave me the child I nursed myself; but when I came to land, and all those young people with me, the king and queen were out walking. The king was very aged, and the queen aged likewise. When I came to converse with them, and the twelve with me, the king and queen began to cry. I asked, " Why are you crying ? "

" Oh, it is for good cause I am crying. As many children as these I should have, and now I am withered, grey, at the end of my life, and I have not one at all."

"Oh, belike you will yet have plenty."

I told him all I went through, and I gave him the child in his hand, and "These are your other children who were stolen from you, whom I am giving to you safe. They are gently reared."

When the king heard who they were he smothered them with kisses and drowned them with tears, and dried them with fine cloths silken and the hair of his own head, and so also did their mother, and great was his welcome for me, as it was I who found them all. And the king said to me, "I will give you your own child, as it is you who have earned him best; but you must come to my court every year, and the child with you, and I will share with you my possessions."

"Oh, I have enough of my own, and after my death I will leave it to the child."

I spent a time, till my visit was over, and I told the king all the troubles I went through, only I said nothing about my wife. And now you have the story.

[*The remainder is from* P. MCGRALE'S *Achill version.*]

And now when you go home, and the slender red champion asks you for news of the death of Anshgayliacht and for the sword of light, tell him the way in which his brother was killed, and say you have the sword; and he will ask the sword from you; and say you to him, "If I promised to bring it to you, I did not promise to bring it for you;" and then throw the sword into the air and it will come back to me.

He went home, and he told the story of the death of Anshgayliacht to the slender red champion, "And here," said he, "is the sword." And the slender red champion asked for the sword, and he said, "If I promised to bring it to you, I did not promise to bring it for you;" and he threw it into the air and it returned to Blue Niall.

THE GHOST AND HIS WIVES.

Narrator, MICHAEL FAHERTY, *Renvyle, co. Galway.*

THERE was a man coming from a funeral, and it chanced as he was coming along by the churchyard he fell in with the head of a man. "It is good and right," said he to himself, "to take that with me and put it in a safe place." He took up the head and laid it in the churchyard. He went on along the road home, and he met a man with the appearance of a gentleman.

"Where were you?" said the gentleman.

"I was at a funeral, and I found the head of a man on the road."

"What did you do with it?" said the gentleman.

"I took it with me, and left it in the churchyard."

"It was well for you," said the gentleman.

"Why so?" said the man.

"That is my head," said he, "and if you did anything out of the way to it, assuredly I would be even with you."

"And how did you lose your head?" said the man.

"I did not lose it at all, but I left it in the place where you found it to see what you would do with it."

"I believe you are a good person" (*i.e.* a fairy), said the man; "and, if so, it would be better for me to be in any other place than in your company."

"Don't be afraid, I won't touch you. I would rather do you a good turn than a bad one."

"I would like that," said the man. "Come home with me till we get our dinner."

They went home together. "Get up," said the man to his wife, "and make our dinner ready for us." The woman got up and made dinner ready for them." When they ate their dinner, "Come," said the man, "till we play a game of cards."

They were playing cards that evening, and he (the gentleman) slept that night in the house; and on the morning of the morrow they ate their breakfast together. When two hours were spent,—

"Come with me," said the gentleman.

"What business have you with me?" said the man.

"That you may see the place I have at home."

They got up and walked together till they

came to the churchyard. " Lift the tombstone,"
said the gentleman. He raised the tombstone
and they went in. " Go down the stairs," said
the gentleman. They went down together till
they came to the door ; and it was opened, and
they went into the kitchen. There were two
old women sitting by the fire. " Rise," said the
gentleman to one of them, " and get dinner ready
for us." She rose and took some small potatoes.

" Have you nothing for us for dinner but that
sort ? " said the gentleman.

" I have not," said the woman.

" As you have not, keep them."

" Rise you," said he to the second woman,
" and get ready dinner for us."

She rose and took some meal and husks.

" Have you nothing for us but that sort ? "

" I have not," said she.

" As you have not, keep them."

He went up the stairs and knocked at a door.
There came out a beautiful woman in a silk dress,
and it ornamented with gold from the sole of her
foot to the crown of her head. She asked him
what he wanted. He asked her if she could get
dinner for himself and the stranger. She said she
could. She laid a dinner before them fit for a
king. And when they had eaten and drunk
plenty, the gentleman asked if he knew the reason
why she was able to give them such a dinner.

"I don't know," said the man; "but tell me if it is your pleasure."

"When I was alive I was married three times, and the first wife I had never gave anything to a poor man except little potatoes; and she must live on them herself till the day of judgment. The second wife, whenever any one asked alms of her, never gave anything but meal and husks; and she will be no better off herself, nor any one else who asks of her, till the day of judgment. The third wife, who got the dinner for us—she could give us everything from the first."

"Why is that?" said the man.

"Because she never spared of anything she had, but would give it to a poor man; and she will have of that kind till the day of judgment."

"Come with me till you see my dwelling," said the gentleman. There were outhouses and stables and woods around the house; and, to speak the truth, he was in the prettiest place ever I saw with my eyes. "Come inside with me," said he to the man; and I was not long within when there came a piper, and he told him to play, and he was not long playing when the house was filled with men and women. They began dancing. When part of the night was spent, I thought I would go and sleep. I arose and went to sleep; and when I awoke in the morning I could see nothing of the house or anything in the place.

THE STORY OF BIOULTACH,

SON OF THE HIGH KING OF ERIN.

Narrator, TERENCE DAVIS, *Renvyle, co. Galway.*

THERE was a king in Erin long ago, and long ago it was. He had a pair of sons, Bioultach and Maunus. Bioultach was the elder. His father took him from school. The son said to him, " Will you give me no more schooling ? "

" I will not give. I think you have enough learning, and I am but poor."

" I give you the quarters of the heaven, of the sea, and of the land, against my body and my soul, that a second meal I will not eat at the one table, that a second night I will not sleep in the one bed, till I go to seek my fortune."

" Oh, my son ! evil is the oath you have taken, and it were better for you to watch over Erin. I think it were worth your while to stay at home, for when you go some other nation will come and cut it off."

" Oh ! it is one to me."

He rose exceeding bright on the morning of the morrow. He rubbed palm to poll and palm to forehead, to make it be seen that he was the best in beauty and in courage. He struck down to the sea. He struck a plank on this side and a plank on that till he made a ship spacious and capacious. He struck on board the ship, and spent four nights and four days, till he landed in Spain without permission.

The King of Spain was out of doors, and he saw the ship coming in without permission. He sent a messenger down to ask who was the champion.

The messenger came back and said to the king, "There is but one man on board, and handsomest of all men that ever I saw is he."

"Oh ! give him an invitation to the court."

The messenger went and gave the invitation. Bioultach spent a day and a year at the court.

"Well," said the king, "you are at my court for a year, and I have never asked who you are."

"If you asked me I would have told you. Bioultach am I, son of the High King of Erin, who left my father's court and pleasant home, since I thought little of the learning he was giving me ; and I think I will stay here no longer."

"I don't know," said the king, "where you will go ; but I believe there is not a place in the world better than Greece, for there is no champion at all, who is a good man, that it is not in Greece he is, in company with the king."

Bioultach took leave of the king, and raised his ship with him, and stopped not till he came to Greece. The King of Greece was on a height (above the sea), and with him a pair of champions —his own son, Splendour, and Splendour-of-the-Sun, son of the King of the Castle of the Stream.

"Go down," said the king to Splendour-of-the-Sun, "and bring me word who is the champion that has come in without permission."

He went down at the command of the king, and saluted the man in the ship. Said he, "The king has sent me to get word who you are."

"Well, I never took from my ship word to give you, unless you get it from me by force."

"I would get it if I had you here."

"I will be there now, but I must secure my ship, that neither storm nor sun may hurt her."

Bioultach went out, and he and the man on shore took hold of each other. Bioultach threw him and tied him tightly, and he fastened the five knots together, and threw him behind him. The king was looking on.

"Go down, Splendour, son of the King of Greece," said he, "and bring me word who is the champion that has tied the other man."

The son of the King of Greece went down, and he and Bioultach took hold of each other, and

Bioultach threw him and tied him more tightly than the other, and laid him along with him. The king had nothing for it but to send a messenger down with a branch of green yew. When Bioultach saw the yew coming, he loosed the men, and the messengers bade him come with them to the palace. Bioultach went with them, and he spent a day and a year with the King of Greece, learning everything the king could teach him, and the king never asked who he was or whence he came. But at the end of a year the king asked,—

"It were good to me to know your name. It was not good to me to put any telling on you ; but now I have a desire you should tell me who you are."

"Oh, I will tell you, and a thousand welcomes. If you asked me at first I would have told you. Bioultach am I, son of the High King of Erin, who left my father's court and pleasant home, since I thought little of the learning he was giving me, and I spent a year with the King of Spain before I came here."

Bioultach had a brother, who was but little when he went away. When he grew big he asked the king,—

"Dada, where went my brother ? "

"I know not," said the king. "I never found out, either by praying or by paying."

"Why did he go away ? "

"Because he thought little of the learning I was giving him."

"I give you the quarters of heaven, of the earth, and of the sea, against my body and my soul, that a second night I will not sleep in one bed, that a second meal at the one table I will not eat, till I go in search of him."

"Oh, my son, evil is the oath you have taken, and it were better for you to stay in Erin, nor leave it altogether without an heir."

"More to me is my brother than all Erin."

When Maunus arose in the morning he took leave of his father, and went down to the sea, and went on board ship, and stopped not till he came to Spain. He spent a day and a year there. The king asked him,—

"Whence are you? I would like to get word of you."

"Oh, you will get it. Maunus am I, son of the High King of Erin, who left the court and pleasant home of my father a year since, yesterday, to search for my brother, Bioultach."

"Oh," said the king, "Bioultach spent a day and year with me here, and if he is alive he is with the King of Greece."

"I will wait no longer till I see him."

"Oh," said the king, "if you reach Greece, do not rise in without permission, for you have no knowledge how to handle a sword."

When Maunus came to Greece he ran in without
permission.   The King of Greece was out of
doors, and Bioultach and Splendour, son of the
King of Greece, and Splendour-of-the-Sun, son of
the King of the Castle of the Stream.

"Oh, Bioultach, to-day it is three years and a
day since you landed, and since then not a ship
has come in without permission, and a ship has
come in without permission to-day. Go down,
Splendour-of-the-Sun, and get me knowledge who
is the champion."

"By my soul, I will not go.   Three years from
to-day Bioultach tied me, and I have never been
well since then."

"Go down, Splendour, and bring me word who
is the champion."

"I will not go.   It was not I whom you told
to go at first.   If it were, I would have gone."

"I believe it is I myself must go."

Splendour-of-the-Sun went down, and he and
the man on board the ship saluted each other.
"Whether you are of the noble or ignoble of
the world, whence are you ?"

"Never from my ship have I given tidings to
tell of me till they were got from me by force."

"Oh! I would do that same if I had you here."

"Oh! it is soon I will be there ; but I must
secure my ship, that sun may not burn nor
shingle hurt her."

Maunus went out, and the two champions took hold of each other. Maunus threw the other, and as he never wrestled with a man before, this is what he made with him—a ball, and he threw him behind him.

"Oh!" said the king, "Splendour, go down now; he is killed yonder."

Splendour, son of the King of Greece, went down, and Maunus tied him as he did the other man; and the king cried to Bioultach, "Thy friendship and thy fealty; let not the sway from Greece, for I have no other but you."

"If you asked me at first I would have gone."

"If I had twelve sons I would send them before you."

"I will go now."

Bioultach went down, and he and Maunus saluted each other.

"Of the noble or ignoble of the world, whence are you?"

"I never from my ship gave tidings to tell of me, unless you take them by force."

"I will take them if I can."

Bioultach and Maunus caught hold of each other, and they spent a long part of the day, and neither of them threw the other. Said Bioultach, "To me it is not good at all to be like this. Let us get swords for each."

"To me it is no worse, if to you it is fine."

"It were good to me if you would tell me who you are."

"I will not tell you.   But if you desire to fight, you will get that."

"It is not good to me to be fighting with you."

"Well, I will not tell you who I am."

Bioultach got a sword, and Maunus another, and they went fighting.   Bioultach was wounding him with the sword, as Maunus did not know how to use it.

"It is not good to me to wound you, and it were good to me if you would tell me who you are.   I could have killed you twice ;   but it is anguish on me to kill you."

"Well, I never held a sword until to-day, and if I am wounded my skill increases ;   and do not spare me, as I will not spare you if I get one chance at you."

They fought for another while.

"Oh ! it was good to me," said Bioultach, "you should tell me who you are, for I do not find it in my heart to be fighting with you."

"Oh," said Maunus, "is it not great the asking you have after my name ?   But do you tell me who you are."

"Oh, I have not hidden my name, ever.   Bioultach am I, son of the High King of Erin, who left my father's court and pleasant home four years and a day since, yesterday."

" Well," said Maunus, " had you a brother ? "

" I had never but one brother, and sorry I am he is not so big as you yet."

" Whether he is big or little, it is he that has been fighting with you since morning."

"Oh," said Bioultach, "it cannot be that you are Maunus."

They embraced one another, and Bioultach was weeping and kissing his brother. When the King of Greece came in among the men—"Oh, Bioultach, what ails you ? "

" My king and my lord, I am fighting with my brother since morning; and if I killed him, I would do nothing but put my sword through my heart."

" Oh, Bioultach, did you not know there was not another man able to fight with you but he ? "

" I thought he was not yet so big."

That was the time Maunus loosed the men, and they were only just alive. The king took them all with him—Bioultach and Maunus, and Splendour son of the King of Greece, and Splendour-of-the-Sun. They went to the court of the High King of Greece.

Bioultach rose in the morning, and he and Maunus went into the garden, and he began to ask Maunus how were his father and his mother and his sister, and how was Erin. But the High King of Greece had a daughter, and she was in

a cloister in the garden. Maunus saw her going
by, as a whiz of wind would go. "Oh, Bioultach,
do you see that beautiful woman?"

"I do not see. She does not concern us.
Perhaps she will never come by again."

"Oh, Bioultach, I have never seen a woman as
beautiful as she."

"Well, you can see her no more. She goes
by only once in a year."

"I shall not live if I don't get another sight of
her."

"Oh! I am sorry I ever saw you; but if you
had an hour of her company you would ask no
more?"

"I would not ask."

Bioultach turned a key in the door, and let in
Maunus, who spent two hours and a-half inside.

"Maunus, are you coming out?"

"Did you not promise me an hour?"

"I have given you two hours and a-half. Be
coming out now."

"I will not come. But I must get that woman
in marriage, or I will not leave a head on you
or on the king."

"Oh, wait patiently till I tell you who she is."

"Make haste and ask her of the king."

Bioultach went in and threw himself on his
knees before the king. "Bioultach," said the
king, "what is it you want? It cannot be that

it is that hard-fortuned daughter of mine that Maunus has seen."

"Oh, it is she; and he says that unless he gets her in marriage he will not leave a head on yourself or on me."

"Can this be possible? But bid him to come in that I may see him and tell him of her doings, and if he is content I will give her to him, and a thousand welcomes; but let him have neither blame nor censure for me or you."

Bioultach went out to Maunus.

"Ha, Bioultach, have you got the woman?"

"I have got. But rise and come to the king, and he will tell you how she has lived."

Maunus went in to the king.

"Ha, Maunus, have you seen that beautiful woman?"

"I have seen."

"You say you must get her in marriage?"

"I must, or I will not leave a stone in the place of your court."

"Well, sit down," said the king, "and I will tell you everything now.

"When she was growing up there came Bocaw More, of Kri-nă-Sorracha, otherwise Shamus Elevayreh, son of the King of Sorracha, and he saw her. He came and asked her in marriage. I refused him. He came again and asked her and I refused. He came the third time and she would not marry him.   He told her he would be even with her.   It was well till two years were over her, and Blue Niall, son of the King of Spain, came here and asked her in marriage.

"I told him what I am telling you.   He said he was content with her.   It was well till they were married, and when they went into their chamber, she never saw sight of him again, nor did any one else.   It was very well till a year passed, and there came Feathery * Clerk, son of the King of the Western World, and asked her in marriage.   I told him what I told the other man.   He said he was content with her.   When they were married and went to sleep, there was no getting him.   She was in the bed, but there was no husband with her.   She would not tell where he went, and we doubted that he could have gone and she not to know where.   When I saw the two fine men were destroyed through her, there came on me a dislike to her, and I made her a dwelling in the garden, and put restrictions on her not to see a man, for I did not like that another man should be destroyed by her.   But now, if you are satisfied, and your brother, so that there will not be blame or censure with you for me if anything happens, I will give her to you and welcome.   Now, Bioultach, I will

* Or Left-handed.   The Irish word means both.

make a house, and I will put bars of iron on it
from ground to roof, and I will put three iron
doors in it, and seven locks on every door. I will
put eight hundred men round it, and Splendour,
my own son, and Splendour-of-the-Sun, and yourself at the three doors before Maunus goes in."

When they were married, and were going into
the fastness, Bioultach said to the king, " I think
it is on the outside the danger will come first, and
I would not like any one to be destroyed but
myself ; I will go on the outer side entirely."

Maunus and his wife went in, and the men
were planted round about the house. Bioultach
went on the outside altogether. The day grew
big with lightning and thunder, and horror came
on the day. When Bioultach saw that the men
were frightened, he ran through them till he came
to the door. He gave his shoulder to the door,
and from door to door he broke till he came
inside. The woman was in bed, and Maunus
was not with her.

"Ha ! my good girl, where is my brother
Maunus gone ? "

" I do not know."

" Tell me where he is gone, quickly."

" Have sense."

" Tell me at once where he is gone."

" Oh, you will never see Maunus again."

" I give you the quarters of heaven, of the

earth, and of the sea, against my body and my soul, that unless you tell me this moment where he is gone I will put my sword through your heart."

" Oh, Bioultach, your friendship and your protection ! I cannot. But, if you are the good champion they say, take a table and place it yonder ; strip yourself, and leave on you nothing but your shirt and trousers. Stand on the table and defend that hole above. If a bar had been put there at first, it would have done the business. But take with you a sword, and I will say you are a good champion if you defend the hole, and I will tell you where Maunus is gone."

Bioultach stripped himself, and went on the table and took a sword. When the man above saw the woman was going to tell the story, " Ha ! my good girl," said he, " are you going to tell the story ? "

" Oh ! don't heed him," said Bioultach ; " but tell the story, and be quick."

" Short is the time since Maunus was here, and now he is in the Bake-house in the east, and three drops on him of the molten torrent, as he had three warnings."

" Oh ! you thief, you wanton, do you desire to tell the story ? "

" My good girl," said Bioultach, " I will defend you."

" When I was growing up," said the woman,
" he asked me in marriage. My father refused
him three times ; and even if he accepted him,
I would not marry him. He said he would be
even with me. When Blue Niall married me he
took him away, and put on him one drop of the
molten torrent, as he had one warning. When,
again, I was married to Feathery Clerk, he took
him away with him, and put on him two drops,
as he had two warnings."

" Oh, you slut, go on with the story no farther ! "
said the big man.

" Do not fear," said Bioultach,—" go on."

" As Maunus got three warnings, on him there
are three drops, and each drop goes to the bone."

It was at this time the king came in through
the men, and he saw Bioultach all red with blood.

" Oh, Bioultach," said he, " you are killed ! "

" I am not. I am coloured with the blood of
the giant, but on myself there is no harm."

" You are a good man, Bioultach," said the
woman ; " I did not believe there was a man in
the world would fight the giant. Now you can
come down."

Bioultach sat down till he told the king. " I
do not know what you will do," said the king.
" But I will get ready a ship, and put on board
eight hundred men of the pick of my kingdom,
and the two champions along with you ; and, on

4

my honour, it is worse to me to part with you
than with them all."

The king fitted out the ship, and he put on board
the two champions and the eight hundred men,
along with Bioultach. When Bioultach went on
board the ship they raised their great sails, speckled,
spotted, red-white, to the top of the mast ; and
he left not a rope unsevered, nor a helm without
* * * * * * in the place where there were seals,
whales, crawling, creeping things, little beasts of
the sea with red mouth, rising on the sole and the
palm of the oar, making fairy music and melody
for themselves, till the sea arose in strong waves,
hushed with magic, hushed with wondrous voices ;
with greatness and beauty was the ship sailing,
till to haven she came and harbour on the coast
of the Land of Brightness.

That was the first place where the giant had his
habitation. Bioultach and the two champions
went out on the shore. " I don't know what we
shall do," said Bioultach ; " but stay, I see a small
little boat coming under great rowing, and in it I
see but one man."

When the boat came to land, there came out
of her a ragged green man, the top of whose
head was out through his old hat, the toes of
his feet through his old boots, his elbows out
through his coat, and his knees through his old
trousers.

" Ha, Bioultach, what likeness of adventure are you putting on yourself to-day ? "

" Bad luck on you! isn't it the same to you what likeness of adventure I am putting on myself ? " said Bioultach.

" Oh, it is not equal. If I were as good as I might be, I should be beside you. But to-day let me go before you."

" I will let you and welcome."

" Leave the other men on board the ship, and we will go to see the giant. I will throw him, and we'll see if you can tie him. But, sorry I am, I can do nothing but throw him."

Bioultach and the ragged green man went into the house, and when the giant saw them he was about to be away. The ragged green man caught him and threw him. Bioultach took hold of him and tied him tightly, and brought the five slenders together, so that the toes of his feet gave conversation to the holes of his ears, and no conversation did they give him but the height of mischief and misfortune.

" Take might and mastery, Bioultach; I thought there was not a man in the world able to tie him."

"Oh, Bioultach," said the giant, "tightly, tightly have you tied me ; ease the fastening a little at the knot."

"Oh, Bioultach," said the ragged green man, "it is better to sell than to buy."

" Oh, Bioultach," said the giant, "do not heed
that thief, but ease the fastening on the cord."

Bioultach laid his hand on the rope, to ease the
knot, and out with the giant through the window,
and out with Bioultach after him. When the
giant was high, Bioultach was low, till the night
came, and Bioultach was forced to sit down, and
he wept his fill. He saw a little light far from
him, and he made for it. When he came in (to
the house) there was a big cat in the ashes, and
she got up and smothered him with the ashes.

" May you be worse a year from to-day," said
he ; and he sat down. It was not long till an old
woman came down to him.

" Ha, Bioultach, it had been better for you to
follow the counsel of the ragged green man than
your own."

" Bad luck to you ! Isn't it all the same to
you whose counsel I follow ? "

" Oh ! it is not the same to me. Not on your
own feet are you going since morning, but on the
enchantments of the giant, and he is sailing a day
and a year's journey from you. But I have here a
little boat of lead, and I will give it to you, and in
whatever place, in the four quarters of the world,
you order it to be, there it will be in the morning.
But you will grant me a request, if you come safe ;
and, if you do not come, I will forgive you."

She gave him a tablecloth : " Every time you

spread it, there will be every kind of food and drink on it ; and fold it when you are done."

"Oh, I will give you any request you ask, if I come safe."

There came then from a room twelve * hags, the ugliest man ever saw.

"Oh, the death-bands on you!" said Bioultach.

"Oh, Bioultach," said the hag, "on us before this was the beauty of youth, but now the decay of age, as on yourself it will yet be. But I hope you will get the better of the giant."

Bioultach took the little boat. "Now, Bioultach, the sea is not far from you. Place the boat on the water, and ask of God and the miracles of the leaden boat that in whatever place is the Bocaw More of the Land of Sorracha you may be there at morning."

Bioultach placed the boat on the water. "I ask of God and the miracles of the leaden boat that in whatever place is the Bocaw More I may be there at morning."

When the day whitened Bioultach was in front of an island, and the haven took fire around him and the boat began to melt. He saw the ragged green man rising from a stone, and he rubbing his eyes after a while of sleeping.

"Oh, Bioultach, you are badly off now, and I must make a gallon to put out the flame."

* Eleven would apparently be the correct number.

" If I am here till you make a gallon, I shall be destroyed."

" I shall not be long away."

It was not long till he came. He threw three palmfuls of water on the flame and put it out.

" Ha, Bioultach, I hope you will not let the giant go to-day. He has no expectation that we will come to-day."

When they went in the giant was about to be off; but the ragged green man caught him and threw him. Bioultach caught him and tied him well, better than he tied him the day before."

" Oh, Bioultach, you have tied me more tightly to-day than yesterday ; but ease the tie a little.''

" It is better to sell than to buy," said the ragged green man.

" Oh, if you are the son of a king by a queen, ease the knot. I am not asking you to set me free."

Bioultach laid his hand to ease him, and away with the giant through the window, and away with Bioultach after him. He was but foolish to seek to get a hold of him. When the night fell Bioultach spread his tablecloth, and every sort of food and drink he wanted was upon it. He ate a great plenty, and he took the boat up. He laid it on the water. " I ask of God and the miracles of my boat that in whatever place is the Bocaw More I may be there in the morning."

He was opposite an island, and the haven froze
round him. It was not long till he saw the
ragged green man coming from the side of a
stone, and he rubbing his eyes.

" Oh, Bioultach, are you frozen there ? "

" And here I shall stay."

"Oh, you will not stay. I will go to the forge
and make an axe to break the (ice)."

He came back, and an axe with him. They
broke the stone of ice. Bioultach came out.
" Now, Bioultach, as we have come on two days
unknown to the giant, he will send out two ball
players, with hurls of gold and balls of silver ;
you will think they are the two champions you
left behind at the Island of the Torrent. If any
limb of their limbs touches you, or the ball, you
are a grey flagstone, and over you heaps of ice
and snow, as big as if you were there for a
hundred years."

When they went up, he saw the two champions
coming. It seemed to him it was Splendour
and Splendour-of-the-Sun were there. They
ran to him, and he was running to them in his
delight. The ragged green man threw them, so
that they failed. They took out the ball. A
man of them struck the ball a blow, and it was
coming straight to Bioultach. He put up his
hand to keep off the ball from his eye. He was
struck on the palm of the hand, and he fell, and

became a grey flagstone, and a holly tree growing through him. When the ragged green man saw that he was destroyed, he bowed down and wept his fill; then he went back to the Island of the Torrent.

"Oh," said the men to him, "is it not long that you have been within? But where is Bioultach?"

"Oh! go ye home. Bioultach is destroyed; he is away from you, a day and a year's voyage before you could reach him. He is a grey flagstone, and over him are heaps of ice and snow."

"We will not go home ever. We have no business at home, but we will be travelling till we get as far as he is."

"Do ye think that together ye could tie the giant?"

"Oh, I do not know."

"Well, I will bring you there in the space of an hour."

He took them with him as far as Bioultach, till they saw him and wept together.

"Let us go in to see the Bocaw More."

When they went in he was conversing with his wife.

"Oh! you have come, and your help is not with you."

"Perhaps you are not a better man than my help."

The ragged green man caught him and threw him. The two champions went to tie him, and he failed them. He sat down.

" Oh, musha, the death-bands on you both! Am I not sorry that ever I left harbour or haven with you? If you two tied him, I would keep a knee on him, and Bioultach would be alive to me at the end of an hour."

" Oh, I think that I could tie him by myself."

The ragged green man threw him, and the two champions went and tied him tightly.

" Oh! ease the knot on me a little."

" You thief! we will not ease."

" Oh, it is the good champions you are," said the ragged green man; "I did not think it was possible to tie him; but you shall see yourselves that I shall have Bioultach now."

He turned to the giant and cut fine pieces of his flesh, till he had the full of his hands, and he ran and squeezed the flesh down on the stone, and Bioultach arose alive again. They smothered him with kisses and drowned him with tears, and dried him with fine cloths silken, and with the hair of their heads; and when Bioultach stooped under the door, the tree that was growing on him fell.

" Oh, Bioultach," said the giant, " tightly, tightly it is they have tied me; but do you ease the tie a little.'

" Oh, you thief ! " said Bioultach, " I will not
ease ; but tell me where is Maunus ? "

" Oh ! he is in the Bake-house outside there.''

" How shall I get him out ? "

" I will put out the flame with a whiff."

Bioultach pulled the giant out, till he quenched
the flame and Maunus came out.

" Where are the other two ? "

" They are inside," said the giant.

" Bring them to me," said Bioultach.

They came out both.

" Can it be lighted when it is empty ? " said
Bioultach.

" Oh, it can," said the giant.

" Kindle it," said Bioultach.

The giant put three whiffs on it, and kindled it.

" Well, I put yourself into it now, and three
drops on you for ever."

" Oh ! Bioultach," said the ragged green man,
" I will forgive you all that ever you did for
putting the giant in.   I was afraid you would not
put him.   But a thousand thanks to God that we
have escaped him."

Bioultach got healing water till he cured them ;
and they went on their way till they came to the
Island of the Torrent, where the eight hundred
men were on board the vessel.

" Oh ! I believe I have forgotten.   I did not go
to the hag.   I must go to her now."

"Will you let me with you?" said the ragged green man.

"I will let you, and welcome. Let us leave the men here!"

Bioultach and the ragged green man went as far as the hag. When Bioultach went into the house, the cat put seven barrels of ashes out of her skin.

"Oh, may you be worse a year from to-day! you are gathering all that since I went away."

Thereupon he sat down, and he did not know where the ragged green man was gone. It was not long till there came to him a beautiful woman, as beautiful as ever he saw, and she said,—

"Oh, Bioultach, thy hundred thousand welcomes! Good be with you. A thousand thanks to God that you accomplished the object of your journey."

"Oh, what good is it to me, when the hag has a request to make of me?"

"Oh, good was the hag herself in the time of your difficulty."

"Oh, I know it is myself she is asking to marry her," said Bioultach.

"Oh! are you certain?" said she.

"Well, I would rather put the sword through my heart than marry her, after seeing you or the like of you."

"Oh! Bioultach, you have your choice. I am

the woman who has the request to make; and
I will release you and bestow on you the boat for
ever, marry or marry me not."

"Oh! I will marry you, and a thousand welcomes. But I don't know where my comrade is
gone. The old clothes that were on him are like
those I see thrown yonder."

" Oh, you will see him, presently."

There came to him eleven women, and he could
not say which of them was the most beautiful.
They sat down, and each one of them gave him
welcome. There came a gentleman, who was
the handsomest he ever saw, and took him by the
hand.

" A hundred thousand welcomes to you,
Bioultach! I am Keeal-an-Iaran, son of the King
of Underwaves, who was under bonds to the
Bocaw More; and my twelve sisters were hags,
as you saw; and I without power to wear any but
old clothes, as you saw. Nor could I raise a hand
against him. But when I saw you coming, I
heard there was not a man to be got as good
as you, and I said it was possible we might get
the better of him. But we would not get the
better of him for ever, only that you let him out
each time. But, the thief! that was the thing was
worst for himself. And now I will go with you
till I leave you safe at home; and my sister, if she
is your choice. And if she is not, she will forgive

you, and a thousand welcomes, as we are released from the hole in the earth where you saw us."

" Oh, I will marry my own wife, and will take her home."

Bioultach, and Keeal-an-Iaran, and the woman went on board the leaden boat till they came to the Island of the Torrent, and they took the eight hundred men and Maunus into the leaden boat. They took Splendour, son of the King of Greece, Splendour-of-the-Sun, son of the King of the Castle of the Stream, Blue Niall, son of the King of Spain, and Feathery Clerk, son of the King of the Western World, on board the leaden boat. The prow to sea they turned, the stern to shore, and they hoisted the great sails, etc., till they came to haven and harbour on the coast of Greece.

The King of Greece was out walking when he saw the hosts making for the court, and he recognised Bioultach.

"Oh, my daughter," said he, "there are three husbands coming to you alive now ; I don't know to which of them you will be."

" Oh, I do not know," said the daughter.

Bioultach came, and all the champions, to the court, and the man of welcome was before them in the king. They passed the night, a third in story-telling, a third in conversation, and a third in soft sleep and deep slumber.

When Maunus arose he asked where was his wife.

" Oh, she is not your wife," said Blue Niall, " but she is my wife."

" Oh, she is my wife," said Feathery Clerk.

By the laws of the land she belonged to Blue Niall.

" Well," said Maunus, " I will make laws for myself. Any man who will not go for a day and a year into the Bake-house, and suffer three drops of the molten torrent, he shall not get the woman. But any man of you two who goes there, he must get the woman and welcome."

" Oh, we will not go there, as we have got ourselves out of it."

" I will go for a year," said Maunus, " but I must get the woman when I come back."

" Oh, we will bestow her on you, but you will not go there, nor any one else that we can keep out of it."

Maunus got the wife ; and they prepared a month's fire and a year's embers, till he and the daughter of the High King of Greece were married together ; and they spent a fortnight after the month in celebrating the wedding with every sort of sport and play. When everything was ended, and each champion was going to his own home, Bioultach said,—

" I believe it is good and right for me to go home to see Erin, and my father and mother."

" Oh, you are settled now."

" Oh," said Keeal-an-Iaran, " I will go with you to see you and my sister in your home."

When Bioultach arose early, full of brightness, he rubbed palm to poll and palm to forehead, to let it be seen that he, as a lion in his valour, was the best in spirit, in beauty, and in courage. He went down to the sea, with his wife and her brother. They bade farewell to the king and the nobles of the court, and went on board the leaden boat. And they hoisted their great sails, etc., till to haven they came and harbour at Binn Edin Vik Shanla, the place where the first ship ever came to Erin.

They found the ford, I the stepping-stones. They were drowned, and I came safe.

KING MANANAUN.

Narrator, P. M'GRALE, *Achill*.

THERE was a king in Erin, whose name was King Mananaun. He was the king of druidism and enchantments and devilscraft. A daughter was born to him, whose name was Pampogue, and she had twelve women attending her, and twelve maids serving her. There was another king in Erin, whose name was King Keeluch, and to him was born a son, whose name was Kaytuch. He took the son to the old wise man, and asked him where he should put his son to learn druidism and devilscraft, so that neither man nor weapon should get victory over him. The old wise man told him to put him with King Mananaun; that he was the best man of druidism to be found. "And a year from this night" (said he) "there was a daughter born to him, and there are twelve women attending her, and twelve maids serving her, and his son would have the same."

There was a third king, whose name was Londu,
son of the King of Gur, and to him a son was
born ; and he also went to the wise old man to
ask him where was the best place to put his son
to learn druidism and devilscraft, and the wise old
man told him to put him with King Mananaun.

The three were going to school together when
Pampogue was sixteen years old, Kaytuch fifteen,
and Londu fourteen. They were coming home
from school, and they went into the smith's
forge ; and Kaytuch took a bar of iron and
twisted it in his hand, and he threw it to Londu,
and told him to straighten it. And he took a
nail and asked the other prince what he would
take to leave his hand on the anvil, and to leave
the nail on his hand, and a blow of the great
sledge-hammer to be struck on the nail ; and (the
other) said he would give it, if he would allow
him a blow without defence in the first battle
between them ; and Kaytuch said he would allow
it, and he drove the nail through the palm of
Londu into the anvil. And she laughed, and
went out and home to her father's house.

When the smith saw what was done in the
forge he asked Londu what he would give him
to loose him. He said that he was a poor gentleman, but that if he ever came into his heirship
he would give him the price of his service. The
smith took hammering with him, and hammered

5

at the top of the nail, and he put something under
the palm and raised it up. He went to the house
of the king and said not a word; but the king
knew all.

In the morning the king wrote to their fathers,
and bade them come to dinner the next day; and
the two kings came and consumed the feast,
and asked was it gold or silver was wanting to
him? if it was they would give it. And he said
it was not, but that there was a dispute between
their two sons, and he would like them to settle
it. "And I know" (said he) "it is jealousy is the
cause." The fathers said that whatever he would
do they were satisfied. "I will open the doors,
and I will put the three inside. Let one man
come out by one door, and the other man by the
other door, and whichever of them she follows,
let her be his."

When the fathers were gone he put the three
into the house and opened the doors, and she
followed Kaytuch. When Londu went out he
saw Kaytuch, and asked if he remembered that
he had a blow without defence to get on him in
their first battle. Kaytuch said, in his opinion
this was no battle.

"No battle at all is there greater than a fight
about a woman."

Kaytuch dropped his hands, and Londu drew
his sword, and cut the head off him. Londu

asked her, " Will you take me now he is dead?"
She refused, and said she would not marry him.
She took Kaytuch and put him in a box, and
herbs of the hill about him. She went then
and fitted out a ship great and gallant, till she
raised the great sails, speckled, spotted, as long,
as high as the top of the mast; and she left not
a rope without breaking, an oar without tearing,
with the crawling, creeping creatures, the little
beasts, the great beasts of the deep sea coming
up on the handle and blade of the oar, till she let
two thirds (of the sail) go, and one third held in,
till the eels were whistling, the froth down, and
the sand above; till she overtook the red wind
of March that was before her, and the red wind
of March that was after did not overtake her;
and she was sailing nine months before she came
to land.

She came near land and cast anchor, and
she saw two men coming, and they carrying
a dead man with them. In the morning the
three were going, and in the evening two were
coming, carrying the dead man again, and it
was like that for three days. One of the men
went out in a currach, and asked her who she
was, or what she was seeking. "If it's a
husband that's wanting to you, come and you
will get one."

She told him to be off, or she would sink

himself and his old currach.*   He went and told
his brothers how she spoke, and the second of
them went and she said the like to him.   Said
the third man " it is like this I have ever found
you."   He went out himself and spoke to her,
and said " God save you, young maiden !   Is it
harm for me to ask who you are, or how far you
are going."

" I will tell you.   But will you tell me ?   Every
evening there are two carrying a dead man, and
three go away alive in the morning."

" I will tell you that, young queen, and welcome.   When my father and mother were living
my father was a king, and when he died, there
came Fawgawns and Blue-men on us, and banished
us out of two islands ; and we are on the top of
the third island with them, and as many of them
as we kill are alive to fight us again in the
morning ; and every day they kill one of us, and
we bring him to life again with the healing
water."

" With me is a champion, the best that ever
struck blow with sword ; and I promise you his
help for a day if you bring him to life."

The man went in, and brought the healing
water, and rubbed it to the wound ; and Kaytuch

* Aarărăx : an old-fashioned currach, without pointed bow
—a square box said to have been used in Achill within the
memory of men now living.

arose alive again ; and he rubbed his eyes with his hands and said " Great was the sleep that was on me " ; and she laughed and told him everything from the time the young king cut his head off. " I took you on board ship, and we were sailing for nine months before we came here ; and I promised your help for a day to this man if he would bring you to life ; but you will not go for a month until you grow strong."

So he and she spent the night together—a third in talking, a third in story-telling, and a third in soft rest and deep slumber, till the whiteness of the day came upon the morrow.

Then he arose and washed his hands and face and ate his breakfast, and went out on the island and came to the house, and asked where they gave battle. Said they to him : " If you were a good champion you would have searched the place, and you would know in what place they give battle."

That made him angry, and he went away and followed the little path that led from the house. He did not go far when he saw the blackness of the hill with people coming towards him. He ran through them as runs a hawk through flocks of wild birds, or a hound through flocks of sheep, till he made a heap of their heads, a heap of their feet, and a heap of their arms and clothes. They would be a prize for him if he thought them any good.

He stretched himself among the dead to see who else was coming. He was not long stretched before he saw an old man and an old woman coming, and a pot and a feather with them ; and they threw a dash on the men on this side and that, and they (were) rising alive like midges. He told them to make no more alive till he killed those they had brought to life. He killed every one of them, and the old man and the old woman ; and the old woman put him under bond to tell the hag of the church that he had killed the Hag of Slaughter and Slaughter himself. He went with himself along the road till he met with a tall, toothless, rusty hag. He asked her if she was the hag of the church ; she said it was she. "I give you notice that I have killed the Hag of Slaughter and Slaughter himself." She gave him a hundred welcomes, and she told him she had been three years in hell to learn druidism and devilscraft ; for it was foretold her that he would come against them that way.

"Go home, and I forgive you." He said he would not go. Said she to him, "Use your sword." He drew a blow of the sword at her and struck her, and there was a dint in the sword that spoiled it for striking, and he put it up in the sheath.

"I forgive you now, and go home." He said he would not go. "Throw me into a hole of water." He threw her; and she was three quarters of an hour in the hole, and he on top of her to keep her down. She got up as fresh as she was before he threw her down.

" I forgive you, Kaytuch."

" I forgive not you."

" Throw me down into a pot of brimstone."

He threw her ; and she was three quarters of an hour in it. She arose as fresh as she was at first. " I forgive you now."

" I forgive not you. Defend yourself now."

He drew his sword on her and struck her, but there was no good in the sword. She put her hands over and took hold of his skin, and put her nails into his blood, and took the full of her fist of his flesh with her. He was about to give up, when the bird spoke to him, to pull her head from its roots. He leaped high, and stood on her shoulders, and took hold of her head, and pulled it from its roots. She put druidism on him then. " Tell the Lamb of Luck that you have killed the Hag of Slaughter and Slaughter himself and the Hag of the Church."

He went along the path, and he came to a great field, and in the field was nothing but a tree, and a big rock of stone, and the lamb. "Are you the Lamb of Luck ? "

" I am."

" I give you notice I have killed the Hag of

Slaughter and Slaughter himself and the Hag of the Church."

The lamb came running to him; and there came near him nothing but the wind, and he fell on the ground; and when he got up he went to the tree, and he and the lamb were running round the tree. He ran from the tree, and leaped round the rock. It was nine perches high and the same in breadth. The lamb leaped through the rock, and put his head into it; and when his head was fastened in the rock, Kaytuch came and cut the head off with his sword. The lamb put him under spells: "Tell the cat of Hoorebrikë * that you have killed the Hag of Slaughter and Slaughter himself and the Lamb of Luck." He met the cat of Hoorebrikë at the edge of a glen, and he asked, "Are you the cat of Hoorebrikë?"

"I am."

He struck a blow of his sword at the cat and split it, and when the sword went through the cat fastened together again. He drew a second blow at the cat, and split it from the snout to the tip of the tail, and the cat fastened again. When he was drawing the third blow, the cat leaped and put the tip of her tail into his side, and there was a barb of poison at the tip of the tail, and it took the heart of Kaytuch out; and

* Explained by the narrator to mean a speckled black and white cat.

Kaytuch took hold of the cat, and thrust his fist into her mouth, and took her heart and entrails out in his hand, and the cat and Kaytuch fell dead.

And one of the three men said, "Let us rise out, and let us help that man." Said another of them, "Oh! it was for a day; let it be for a day, and him do the work of the day himself; that they would go to help him on the next day." They rose out and went with themselves after him, and as they were going they found the slaughter made, till they came and found himself and the cat killed. They took hold of the heart and insides that were in his fist, and put them into his belly again. They rubbed the healing water on him, and he was as well as he was ever before.

They went with themselves, and there came a gust of wind and stirred a wisp, and the cat ran and struck her foot on the wisp. They said it was the cat's heart they put into him in place of his own; and one of them went forward, and drew his sword, and cut his head off again. They took the cat's heart out, and put his own heart in again, and rubbed the healing water on him, and he was as well as he was at first.

When they came home they had a pleasant night—three-thirds of the night : one-third in talking, one-third in story-telling, and a third in soft rest and deep slumber. Then came the three brothers in their arms to Kaytuch, and (asked) him to be king in their father's place, and they themselves would be his messengers. He said he would not ask their property from them, but it should remain with themselves. They asked him to divide the property between them. He gave the first island to the eldest, the second island to the second, and the island they were on to the youngest son. When Kaytuch parted from them, they gave him everything they had as a present. And Kaytuch and his wife, having taken farewell, went from the island for Erin.

When they came to Erin, the place where they made haven and harbour was beneath the house of Finn McCool. Finn sent one of his men and told him he would give him five pounds and a suit of clothes if he brought him word who the man was. Conan went and asked him, "Who are you? My master sent me to see, and said he would give me five pounds and a suit of clothes for bringing him word who you are."

Kaytuch laid hold on him and bound him, and threw him under the molten torrent, in a place where every drop would go from the fat to the marrow, and from the marrow to the inmost marrow, and left him there. When Finn saw what he did, he sent Keeltje to him; and Keeltje saluted him, and spoke to him politely, and asked him to tell him, if it were his honour's pleasure, who he was, that he might tell Finn.

"Tell Finn I will be with him for dinner." Then he released Conan, and told him never to bring a message again to a gentleman.

Then he went part of the way with his wife, till he put her near her father's house, and he returned to Finn. Then they ate their dinner, and they went out hunting. Kaytuch said he was a stranger, and that he would take a glen to himself. And he took a glen to himself; and as he was killing, he threw the game on the road, until he said it was time for him to go home. He tied the birds together, and made a bundle of them, until Finn and his hosts came, and he told them to take up the burden, but they were not able to raise the burden. He put the tip of his boot under it, and threw it over his shoulder, and ran home; and Keeltje ran after him, and Kaytuch had his dinner eaten when Keeltje came, and they were together till morning. The second day they went hunting, and Kaytuch went this day to the glen they had the day before, and they had had but two birds of that glen, but he had the same burden. And the third day the like happened; and on the fourth day there came a great mist on them, and they knew not where they were going, and they went into a great castle, and there was food on the table, and they sat down and were eating; and there came the shadow of a woman and took away the broken food, and laid more food on the table until they had eaten enough. Then there was a bed for every two, and a bed for Kaytuch and a bed for Finn. Then the young girl herself showed another bed, and told the kings to go down to the young girl ; but Kaytuch said he had a wife already, but that Finn had no wife, and for him to go down. Finn went to her, and spoke to her ; and she said that if he would give her the amber bracelet belonging to the daughter of the Blauheen Bloyë, in the eastern world, he could come into the bed to her. So he went into the bed, and was with her till morning.

On the morning of the morrow Kaytuch and Finn went to dinner to the house of King Mananaun, and there was great welcome for them, and mighty rejoicing that Kaytuch was come back alive to them. They prepared a great dinner for them, and when it was ready they sat down to eat, and Finn took his knife and fork and laid them on the food, and said he would not eat a bit until Pampogue granted him a request.

" I will grant you any request, except to let my husband go to fight with the Blauheen Bloyë."

"Unless you grant me that, I will not eat any food."

"Sooner than you should be without eating, I will grant you even that.'

And when Kaytuch saw he was to go, he rose and threw his knife and fork from his hands, and he went with himself, and Finn followed him. And Pampogue followed Finn, and asked of him one favour, to bring her husband back to her, dead or alive; and if he were alive, to hoist the grey-green sails, and, if dead, the red.

Kaytuch and Finn and the Feni went to go the land of the eastern world, to the place where was the Blauheen Bloyë. And when they came to harbour they secured the ship, and Kaytuch went to the door of the Blauheen Bloyë, and knocked at the Cora Conra (? the knocker), and he was asked what he wanted. And he said, a house. And they said there was a house below, and in it were owas, and he was to go and take it. He went into that house, and the big owas began to laugh and the little owas began to cry; and he asked them the cause; and the big owas said they would have a bit off him, and the little owas said there would not be one bit for them to get. And every one of them got up and put a bolt on the door, and he put bolt and latch on the door; and he caught hold of one of the owas by the foot, and struck another with him, and he was killing till he killed the last man of them. And he rose out to see if Finn and his men were coming, and they were drawing near, twelve of the Feni, and the twelve could not throw out one man of the dead men. He took hold of them and threw them out.

Then he went to the criers of the kitchen, and knocked at the door, and was asked what he sought. He said he was seeking food. They told him to go into the field and kill an ox. He went and he saw a bull, and the bull ran at him, and he ran away, and came into the house, and the bull followed him in, and he ran and closed the two doors, and he had the bull inside. He killed him and skinned him, and went out to see if his people were coming, and they came into the house, but they were not able to carry a quarter of the bull. He put the four quarters into the skin and carried them home.

He went again to the criers of the kitchen, and he was asked, "What are you seeking now?"

"I am seeking turf to make a fire."

"There is a stack outside, and take what you want."

There was devilment in everything. He ran and took hold of the turf stack, and put his hands down and pulled out some of the turf, and ran as well as he could, and the turf was running after him to the door to smother him. Then he knocked for the keepers of the kitchen, and asked them for the making of a bed, and they told him

to take what he wanted from the haggard ; and
he went and put his back to the haggard, and
pulled out some of the straw, and the straw
ran after him to the door to smother him, but
he ran from the haggard.   He went again to the
criers of the kitchen, and they asked him
what he was looking for.   He said he was
looking for water.

 " There is a well outside, and take what you
want of it."

He went to the well and put his hands into the
water, and took up some of it with him, and
the water was running after him in the hope of
drowning him, but he ran from it.   Then again
he knocked for the criers of the kitchen, and
they asked him, " What are you looking for
now ? "

" Fire," said he, " and a pot."

 " Go to the house of the owas, Oramach ; * there
is fire and a pot there, and take them with you."

He went into the house of the owas, Oramach,
and the owas gave a laugh, and said the boiler
was not cooking the meat for want of fire, and
he would boil it with his head.   And the two
caught hold of each other in the keen, close
clutches of wrestling.   If you were to go seeking
for fun from the west of the world to the fresh-

---

* Possibly identical with the Amhas (pron. *owas*), Ormanach
of Campbell's " Connal Gulban."

ness of the world, it is to that pair you would
betake yourself. They made hard of the soft,
and soft of the hard, till Kaytuch gave him a
squeeze down, and put him on his knees; and
he put his head down on the fire, and kept it
there till the flesh was cooked. He took the
pot with him, and the flesh, and he himself and
Finn had enough to eat; and he told the other
people who were with him to prepare for themselves and eat. And he asked them to give
him leave to sleep, and for them to keep watch.
Then he slept. And what woke him but their
snoring in their sleep? He rose out, and saw
hundreds of people coming, and with them tarred
wood and straw to set fire to the house. And
Kaytuch killed them all, and went into the house
and woke the others, and bade them keep better
watch. He went to sleep, and slept not long till
he woke again, and they asleep; and he rose out
and saw (people) coming the second time as they
came first; then he ran forward and killed them
again, and he did that four times during the
night. In the morning, when the day rose, he
went to the criers of the kitchen, and knocked
at the door, and they asked him what he
was wanting. He said to them, "Three hundred men in front of me, three hundred behind
me, three hundred on each side of me, and
three hundred on each edge of my sword's

edges." And he had that on the spot. He ran through them as runs a hawk through flocks of birds, or a dog through flocks of sheep, till he made a heap of their heads, a heap of their feet, a heap of their arms and clothes. If they were a good prize they were no profit. And again he knocked for the criers of the kitchen, and he asked for six hundred men in front, six hundred behind, six hundred on each side, and six hundred on each edge of his sword's edges. And he had them on the spot, and he did to them as to the first. And then he asked for nine hundred, and treated them in the same way. And he knocked again, and Brailskë More said he would go himself to battle, and it was three hours before he killed the Brailskë. The Blauheen Bloyë arose, and said it was a pity he did not go himself to battle at first, before his men were all killed. And Kaytuch and he went to fight on the ground, and the battle began between them till Kaytuch killed him.

And he went into the house to the daughter, and she asked him where was he going, the man who killed her father and his hosts?

"Am I not a better man for you than all of them?"

"If I had known that it was to me you were drawing, I myself would have helped you."

The two went into bed, and he took from her

6

the amber bracelet, and was going. She asked him would he not stay with her, and he said he would not; and he went to Finn, and they prepared to go home.

When they went on board ship, he told Finn he was to be killed that day. He said he was two-and-twenty-years old that day. "The man that killed me at first is to kill me again to-day. He will come as a bird in the air, and will put the same form on himself as mine, and I will ask him to come up on board the vessel, and there will be a great battle between myself and Londu."

Londu came on board the vessel. His apprenticeship was over that day, and he was cousin to the woman whom Kaytuch had treated so, and taken the amber bracelet from her. The two went to battle on board the ship. They began young like two little boys (and fought) until they were two old men. They fought from being two young pups until they were two old dogs; from being two young bulls until they were two old bulls; from being two young stallions till they were two old stallions. Then they began a battle in the shape of birds; and they were fighting as two hawks, and one of them killed the other. The one that was below struck the one that was above, and as the first one fell dead, he killed the other in falling on him; and it was Londu, son of the king of Gur, that fell first. And he was thrown out into the sea, and the other was brought home to the wife of Kaytuch, son of the king, Keelach. When they came to harbour they raised the grey-green * sails, and when they landed Kaytuch's wife was there before them; and they gave her the bird, and she said that was what she was to get in place of her husband. She wept bitterly, and she with the bird, and Finn and the Feni went home and gave her no heed. Then she saw two birds fighting in the air, and one of them killed the other. And birds came and put leaves of a tree on the bird that was killed; and it was a half-hour of the clock, and (the bird) arose alive again. And she put the leaves on her own bird, and then there was half an hour of the clock, and the bird arose alive to her again. And he asked her if she had got the amber bracelet from Finn; and she said she did not get it. Then she and he went to her father's house, and there was an invitation proclaimed for nine nights and nine days for eating and drinking in the house of King Mananaun, with exceeding joy that Kaytuch was come to them safe out of every battle. And the priest came and the pair were married. And Finn went to the woman who put the obligation on him to bring her the amber bracelet; and he

---

* This is not in accordance with the directions given. The red sails ought to have been up.

asked her and said to her, " If I promised to bring it *to* you, I did not promise to bring it *for* you, and I will not give it to you." So he gave it to the wife of Kaytuch when he heard he was alive again.

And when everything was finished I had nothing after them but shoes of paper and stockings of buttermilk ; and I threw them to themselves, till I came home to you to the village of Kill-da-veac and Kill-da-woor, to the little turf bog, to the village where I was born, to the village at the beginning of week, till I fired the shot of a gun frilsjke, frælsjke, kipini, qropaanax ; till I killed Londu, and the qaanăx, till I got the load of thirty horses of marrow I took out of the body of the king of the wrens.*

---

* These nonsense endings frequently contain untranslatable words. I give these in the phonetic spelling : but I should add that qaanăx means, probably, a kind of wild goose. Londu mean " blackbird " kipini, sticks, or dibbles used for planting.

THE CHAMPION OF THE RED BELT.

Narrator, P. MINAHAN, *Malinmore, Glencolumkille,
co. Donegal.*

THERE was a king and a queen, and they
had three sons. She died with the third.
The king married another queen. She had ill-
feeling towards the children. The king had no
rest till he would banish the children. She took
to her bed and would not live if he would not do
something or other with them. He went to an
old man who was in the town. He told him in
what way he was. The old man told him to get a
barrel made and to put the children into it. " Put
a red belt on one and a black belt on the other."

He got the barrel made, and an air-hole in it,
and a weight for ballast, to keep it from rolling.
He put the children into the barrel then. He
put two swords with them. He put them out
on the sea. The barrel was going before the
wind till it came under the court and castle of
the King of Greece.

The king had a herdsman; the herdsman was
herding cows. The king had one cow, and she
was troublesome minding, licking the stones that
were on the shore. There was seaweed growing
on the stones. He ran down to the cow. He
came to the stone. He saw a white spot on the
stone. He kept looking at the stone, and he saw
that it was wood was in it. He tumbled it and
cut the end out of it. He found two children
and two swords. He put his hand down into
the barrel. He took up the two children. He
never saw two that were so fair as they. He
took the two children home. He said it was
Providence sent them to him.

They were with him. When he would hear
anyone coming into his house, he ordered the
children out of the room. It was told the king
that the herdsman had two children (found) in a
barrel on the shore. The king was not willing
to believe it. He said he would go himself to
the herdsman. He went to him. He asked him
if he found two children. The herdsman said he
did not find. " If you have found them," said
the king, " do not conceal them from me."

He said he had found. He told the children
to come down out of the room. They came down
to the king. The king took hold of the children
with his hands. He viewed them. " Well," said
the king, " wherever it is the children have come

from, there is royal blood in them." The king had no child but one little girl.

"Give me the children. I will give them better care than you. I will support yourself and your old woman as long as you are alive."

He could not refuse. The king took the children with him. He cared for them till they grew to be young men. The king's daughter thought they were her brothers. The king put learning on them. They were the two champions. They were fowling every day that was fine. At that time there was a great hurling match to come off. The King of Lochlann sent a challenge to the King of Greece for a hurling match, kingdom to be staked against kingdom. There was a pretty strand under the court and castle of the King of Greece. When the day of the hurling match came, the King of Greece ordered the two champions to go hunting. They went hunting. They were not long gone from the house when they met five young men, every one of them with a hurling stick. "I don't know where they can be going," said the champion of the red belt.

"I don't know," said the champion of the black belt. They saw five others coming the same way. He said to one of them he wondered where they were going. "I will tell you ; and it is a great wonder that you are going fowling to-day."

"Why is that?" said the champion. "I believe you have heard all about it yourself."

"I have heard nothing."

"The kingdom of your father is staked against the kingdom of the King of Lochlann in a hurling match to-day. We are going to the hurling match on behalf of your father."

They returned home. They said to the King of Greece they would not lose his kingdom, but would play on his behalf. They threw off their hunting suits. They put on light suits for running. They got two hurls. They went to the strand. There was a great crowd on the strand. The ball was going out. There were twenty-four men on each side. They said their father's kingdom should not be lost, that they would play on his behalf. Two were then put out, and they were put then in their place. There were riders keeping the strand clear. The ball was put in the middle of the strand down in the sand. The forty-eight men came round the ball. The champion of the red belt got the ball. He struck it. When it fell again he was shaking it, and he struck it again. He sent it to the other end. He said to the King of Lochlann that his kingdom was lost. The King of Lochlann said his men had not got fair play in the hurling. "I will give you fair play," said the champion of the red belt; "myself and my brother to hurl against your four-and-twenty; and this is the bargain I'll make with you:—Whoever it is that sends the ball to the goal is to have a blow with his hurl on the others: if your four-and-twenty men win the goal against us, they have four-and-twenty blows to strike on us. If we win the goal, we have a blow on every one of them."

The ball was put in the sand. They gathered round it. The champion of the red belt had the ball. He struck it. When it fell he was shaking it again. Not one man on the strand got a blow at it till he put it to the goal.

"Now," said he, "did you not get fair play?"

"I got it; you are the best champion ever I saw."

"Put the men in a row that I may get my blows."

He put the men standing in a row. "Now," said he to his brother, "any man that I don't knock down, knock him down you."

He struck the first blow. He killed. He struck the second blow then. He killed. He was striking and killing. There was one man at the end outside. When he came killing, drawing towards him, he went out of the row. He went up on the side of a hill.

"Death and destruction and the death-bands on you, champion of the red belt! It is you that are doing the slaughter on this strand to-day. Don't you know what country you came out of ?—that it is out of a two-ended barrel you came in to the court and castle of the King of Greece?"

"Sit down, and wait till I come to you."

"I will not wait. I saw you killing many a one. Perhaps you will kill me."

"My word to you, I will not touch you till you tell me about the barrel."

"I will take your word."

He went up then till he came to the place where he was sitting. "What is it you say about the barrel?"

"It is a two-ended barrel the old man found by the sea. He took you out of the barrel; he took you home. The king heard he had found two children in the barrel. He did not believe it. He went down to the old man to see if he had found them. The old man said he had. He brought down the youngsters. The king sat down. He took hold of them by the hand. He viewed them. He said they had royal blood."

"'Give me the children. I will care for them better than you.'

"'It is hard for me to give them from me.'

"He could not refuse the king. The king said he would not let them have a day of want. 'I will support you and your old woman as long as you are alive.'

" The King of Greece is not your father," said the man. " He had no family but the one young girl in the house."

" I am grateful to you for all that you have told me about the way I came here. If I live, I will do you a service."

They were troubled. They knew not whence they had come. They went home. The King of Greece welcomed his two sons.

" Put not your sonship upon us. We are only the children of a poor man who had no means to rear us. I will sleep no night but this night in your house till I find out how I came hither."

" Do not so," said the king ; " stay in this place. I will give you the half of my kingdom."

" I would not stay if you gave me your kingdom all."

When the king's daughter heard he was not her brother, she was ready to die unless he married her. He said to her he would not marry her ; that he would wear his two legs down to his two knees till he found out how he came. " If I find that out, I will come to you and marry you."

They were greatly troubled when they were departing. They went till they came to the sea. He threw his hat out. He made a ship of the hat, a mast of his stick, a flag of his shirt. He hoisted the sails speckled spotted, to the top of the straight mast. He turned the prow to sea, the stern to shore, and he left not a rope without breaking, nor a cable without rending, till he was listening to the blowing of the seals and the roaring of the great beasts, to the screams of the seagulls ; till the little red-mouthed fishes were rising on the sole and the palm of the oars ; till they steered the vessel in under court and castle of the King of the Underwaveland.

They put fastening on the ship. They went on the land. They were going with themselves. There was no one at all coming towards them. They were all going one way, so that there was a great crowd where they were stopping. Said the brother, " Perhaps you will find some one in the crowd to tell you how we came " (*i.e.*, our origin).

They went on with themselves. A man met them. They asked him what was the cause why the people on the island were all going one way.

" It has happened you were not reared in the island when you do not know the reason of the people's going. The King of Underwaveland has but one daughter. She is going to be married to-morrow to the son of the King of the Eastern World. There is an invitation to the wedding to all the island. There are open cellars. There is eating and drinking to all that come."

They went on till they came to the king's house. There was a great crowd there. They were strangers in it. No one gave them any heed.

No one was there without an invitation except themselves.

"Stand at the door behind," said the champion of the red belt to his brother ; " I will stand at this door."

No one went in or out that they did not strike. They were killing them. The king got word there were two blackguards at the door who were killing numbers of people. The king rose out. He said he thought there was not a blackguard at all in the crowd ; that there was eating and drinking for every one to get. The champion of the red belt said they were not blackguards at all ; they were two strangers on the island ; they would demean themselves by coming uninvited. The king bowed to them and gave them an invitation. He would invite (he said) any company in which they were.

He drew them into the parlour. The bride was there getting ready for the marriage. She and her mother began to converse. The bride said that if she knew he had no wife, she would not marry a man but him. The mother told the king what the bride said. The king told the champion of the red belt what the bride said. The champion of the red belt said, " I have a wife. My brother is single ; and if it is her will to marry him, I am satisfied."

She sent a letter to the son of the King of the Eastern World that she had a husband she preferred to him. He sent a letter to her that he would not give up his wife to any man, without his fighting for her. The champion of the black belt sent a letter to him that he would fight at midday on the morrow, in such and such a place. When the morrow came the champion of the black belt washed himself for the fight. He told the champion of the red belt to take care of the woman till he came back. He went then. He was going up the road. He met an old red man sitting by the road side. He had a great harp, and he was playing on it. He asked the champion of the black belt to sit down while he played him a tune. He said he had no time, that he was going to battle ; but the old man told him to stand a little while till he played him one tune. He stood a while ; the first strain the old man played, he fell asleep. He was sleeping there then till the son of the King of the Eastern World came. He jumped down from his carriage, and cut his head off. He went riding back. The champion of the red belt knew nothing till he came to the hall door.

" My brother is killed," said he ; "short it is till I kill you."

" Don't do that," said the bride; " leave it to me to do."

" If you don't do it I will destroy the island."

The son of the King of the Eastern World

came up to the hall door.   She rose out.   She
caught him by the hand.   He said he was fatigued
after the battle.   They went into the house.   She
opened a cupboard ;   she gave him a cup of
drink.   He drank her health.   When he raised
the cup of drink he bent his head backwards.
She drew a sword from under her apron.   She
lopped the head from him.

" If you had not been so quick doing it, I
would have done the same to you as to him," said
the champion of the red belt.

He went then to the place where his brother
was killed.   When he came to it he was troubled.
There came a lump of mist out of the head.
Some one spoke to him out of the mist :

" Go to the Eastern World ;   the children of
Kanikinn have a bottle of the water of healing
that brings the dead to life."

It put great joy on him.   He went then towards
the Eastern World.   He could get no information
of it.   He then went on three days.   He could
get no information of it.   Then he went on for
three days more.   Every one had information to
give him then.   An old man was putting bad
spirits on him.

" There is a yard around the court ten feet
high.   It is written on the gate : " If you go in
you will never come out alive."

He went up to the gate.   He cleared it at a

leap. There were three sons of Kanikinn in an alley playing ball. They spied the champion coming in the gate. Said one of the young men,

"You have come in very nimbly; not so nimbly will you go out."

"He will go," said the eldest; "any champion who could make that leap is a gentleman. Don't speak an angry word till I permit."

The champion of the red belt then came forward and saluted them as politely as he could. He told them how things were with him; that he had come there to seek the bottle of the water of healing that made the dead alive.

"Well!" said the other, "there is ill luck on you. The king knight of the black castle took that bottle from me seven years ago. There is not a day he does not kill three hundred men, and it is better for you to tarry here with me; I will give you a third of my possessions, for I fear he will kill you."

"I am thankful to you for your kindness: since I have come so far I will go to meet him whether I live or die."

He asked was there any short way at all to the castle. He showed him a short way. He said farewell. He went on till he came to the gate, till he cleared the gate out with a leap. He was going with himself then for a while till he saw the black castle. He went into the yard.

He could see no one. He feared to go in. Night was coming, and he went in, whether he was to live or die. There was no one within, but the house was full of feathers. He said it was like a slaughter-house. He heard a loud sound coming into the house. He was startled. There was a barrel at the side of the house. He went behind it. Then the light burst from the door, and the king knight of the black castle came. He hung his sword on a peg. The blood was dripping from the tip of it. He had on a coat of steel. He went to put off the coat. The champion of the red belt rose from behind the barrel. "If that is your fighting suit, do not put it off you till you fight with me."

Said the king knight of the black castle, "It is a man without life you are. I am only after drawing my sword out of the last man of three hundred, but I will not fight you till morning. If it is lodging for the night you want, you will get it."

"That is what I want."

"Don't be afraid. I will not touch you till morning."

The king knight of the black castle set to till he lighted the fire with sticks and faggots. He told the other to sit near the fire. The champion of the red belt was watching the door. He asked him was there any one there except himself. The king knight of the black castle

7

said there was not; "and great joy is there on me to have you here to-night. I have talked with no one for seven years."

The champion of the red belt said he had heard that there was with him a bottle of the water of healing, that made the dead alive; that his brother was killed. Would he give him the loan of the bottle?

"I have not got the bottle. That is the bottle that makes people alive. My stepmother took it from me seven years ago. There is not a day I don't kill three hundred men, and my stepmother brings them to life again. A hag of sorceries she turned out, to put pains on me, that they will never be killed for me, while I live; and but that providence puts strength in my heart, I would not get the better of them."

When they took their supper the champion of the red belt asked him, "Have you any one at all but yourself?"

"No," said the king knight of the black castle. Then he asked if he had been brought up on the island. He said, "Not he; that it was a son of the King of Erin was in it; that his mother died when he was born; that the king married another queen."

"Were there any other (children) but your-self?" said the champion of the red belt.

"There were two other brothers."

" Are they alive ? "

" Oh ! I think not.   They were put in a two-ended barrel."

" Did you hear that your father put any mark on them ? "

" He said he put a red belt on one, a black belt on the other."

" True it is ; people meet and the hills meet not.   I am your brother ; but the champion of the black belt is dead."

He stripped and showed him the belt.   The two fell into an embrace.   Then they went to rest. When the day came on the morrow the king knight of the black castle rose.   He told his brother not to rise, as he was tired, before breakfast was ready.   Then he got up and washed himself. They took their breakfast.   The king knight of the black castle said it was a pity he could not stop during the day to keep him company.

" Stay here, you, till I go and do my sufficiency of killing as quickly as I can."

" What would you think if I went in your place to-day ? "

" It would be no use for you to go with only the strength providence has given you.   You would not get the better of them."

Said the champion of the red belt, " We are two brothers.   It is a poor thing for me if I can't kill for one day what you are killing for seven years."

The champion of the red belt took his sword. The other was not satisfied at all to let him go. He would not stay on his advice.

"Put on my suit of steel; I could not do much without that."

"I will not put it on. Unless I fight in the suit that's on me, I am beaten."

He went till he came to the three hundred men. He asked them if they were ready. They said they were. When they saw the little man coming they were laughing and mocking him. He went straight in through them. He made heaps of their heads and their feet, a prize of their arms and their clothes. When he killed the three hundred, he stood up. He said what was the good of killing them, and they to be alive again in the morning? Then he lay down among the dead men to see what it was brought them to life. There came a hag, with one leg out of her haunch, one eye in her forehead, a bottle of the water of healing on a button that was on her breast. There was a feather in the bottle. She rubbed the feather on the first man she came to. She made nine of them alive. The champion of the red belt arose and killed the nine. Then he and the one-legged hag struck together. They were fighting a long time. He got angry that he was wasting the day. He lopped the head off her. He took the bottle that was hanging on her breast. He hung it on the button that was on his coat. Then said the hag, when she was falling,—

" I lay on thee the spells of the art of the druid, to be feeble in strength as a woman in travail, in the place of the camp or the battle, if you go not to meet three hundred cats. Tell them you have slain three hundred men and the one-legged hag."

He went forward then till he came to the three hundred cats. He cried out to them that he had killed three hundred men and the one-legged hag.

Said they : " It is dearly you will pay for that."

He and the cats went to battle. The cats leaped above him. He made a rush at them. He was killing them as fast as he could, till he killed them all but the great old speckled cat. Said she when she was falling,—

"I lay on thee the spells of the art of the druid, to be feeble in strength as a woman in travail, in the place of the camp and the battle, if you go not to fight the Wether of Fuerish Fwee-erë. Tell him you have slain three hundred men, three hundred cats, and the one-legged hag."

He went forward in the camp. He and the Wether of Fuerish Fwee-erë went to battle. He came behind him to come on him with a run to kill him. He missed him the first time. He went behind him again. He came at him with a run. When the champion of the red belt saw the Wether approaching him, he made ready not to miss him: The Wether came forward. The champion of the red belt put the sword through his heart. Said he, when he was falling,—

"I lay on thee the spells of the art of the druid, to be feeble in strength as a woman in travail, in the camp and the battle, till thou goest to meet the king cat of the Western Island. Tell him you have slain three hundred men, and three hundred cats, and the one-legged hag, and the Wether of Fuerish Fwee-erë."

He went forward in the camp. He met the king cat of the Western Island.

"Death on you! Short is your own life now. Little I thought I was not done with you the day that I put you in the barrel."

"Hideous hag! I am stronger to-day than I was that day."

He and the hag struck together, till he made hard of the soft, and soft of the hard, and (made) the fresh-water wells in the middle of the grey stones. From the hollows of the world to the heights of the world they came to look on at the fight was between them.

She had a long tail. There was a poison spot on the tail. There was a great claw at the tip of the tail. She rose on high. She came down on his head. He met her with the sword. She curved her tail and put the claw in his hand. He was bleeding. The day was hot and he was bleeding greatly. Down she came with a slap. She put the poison spot through his heart. She got the claw fixed in his heart. She drew out his heart on his side. When the man was falling, the cat opened her mouth as wide as she could with the rage that was on her ; and when he saw her mouth open, and he falling, he thrust his hand into her mouth and pulled out her heart. The two fell dead. They were lying dead then.

The king knight of the black castle was troubled that he let his brother go to fight in his place. He went on his track to see how he was doing. He went forward in the camp. He found the three hundred men killed. He went forward farther in the camp. He found the one-legged hag killed. He went still forward in the camp. He found the three hundred cats killed. He went still forward in the camp. He found the Wether of Fuerish Fwee-erë killed. He went on and found his brother and his stepmother killed. Then he did not know what to do. He was afraid lest he might put the cat's heart into the man ; for the evil temper of the cat might drive the man mad and kill him. The lump of mist came. It spoke to him : " Is it not easy for you to distinguish between the big heart of the man and the little heart of the cat ? "

He took up the big heart. He washed it and fixed it in his brother. He found the bottle of the water of healing that was hanging on his brother. He dipped a feather in the bottle and rubbed it to his brother's mouth. His brother arose alive.

" I seem as if I was asleep."

" Did you not wonder then ? It was providence saved me when I did not come to battle with you on the night when you rose up from behind the barrel, or you would have killed me as you have done (to the others) to-day."

" What good is it for you to be big when you are not a good soldier ? "

" It is long since I have had time any day to kill birds. Many's the time I was hungry when I killed the three hundred men. I had no time to kill birds for my breakfast in the morning. To-day I have time to kill plenty."

" You will not kill a beast to-day," said the champion of the red belt.

He then went killing. He killed. The big man went among the gathering of the birds. He was killing till night. He said he had enough killed.

Then they went home. They got ready their supper. They took their supper. They went to rest them. The king knight of the black castle was not going to rise very early. He had nothing to kill.

They were going to take a walk in the wood. " Is there a woman at all who is good for much on the island ? " said the champion of the red belt.

"There is a king's daughter on the island, and I think I would get her in marriage."

He and his brother went to the king's house. He got the king's daughter in marriage. Came the priest of the pattens and the clerk of the bell. The pair were married. The wedding lasted nine nights and nine days. He took her home then. They stayed at home a couple of days until he rested.

"Now," said the champion of the red belt, "you have a wife; it is time for me to go to my brother to make him alive."

"I will be with you," said the king knight of the black castle.

They came to his brother. He made his brother alive as well as ever he was. They went to the house of the King of Underwaveland. There was great joy on the bride to see her husband. Came the priest of the pattens and the clerk of the bell. The pair were married.

"Now," said the champion of the red belt, "you have both your wives. It is right for you to go with me till I get my wife."

They went on then to the island of the King of Greece. When the daughter of the King of Greece saw the champion of the red belt there was great joy on her. They told the King of Greece what their birth was. Came the priest of the pattens and the clerk of the bell. The pair were married. The wedding lasted nine nights and nine days.

JACK.

Narrator, P. MINAHAN, *of Malinmore, Glencolumkille,*
co. Donegal.

THERE was a master, and he went to look for
a servant boy. He fell in with Jack. He
hired him. He took him home. On the morning
of the morrow the master was leaving home. Jack
asked him what he should do that day.

"Go threshing in the barn," said the master.

"Shall I thresh anything but what is there?"

"Do not," said the master. "If you thresh all
that's there, thresh no more."

"What'll I go to do then?" said Jack.

"Don't do a turn till night."

The master went away then, and Jack went
to the barn and began threshing. The chaff
began flying about, and he slashed through the
barn, and there was not a grain of it left in
an hour by the watch. Jack cleared the barn.
He shook the straw. He cleaned up the barn.
He went into the house and sat down by the

fire. The mistress bade him bring in a basket of turf. He said he would not. "You won't be there," said the mistress, "unless you do some work."

"I won't do one turn till night."

"Musha, you won't be there," said the mistress.

The two quarrelled. She put him out of the house. He went out and stayed about the place till night.

When Jack went out a neighbour came in. The mistress got dinner for him. When he was going, she went with him part of the way. They came to an old lime-kiln. They went into it. He kissed the mistress. Jack was watching them always. "If I knew," said she, "where you would be working to-morrow, I would bring you your dinner."

"I'll be at work ploughing at the east end of the village. I'll have a white horse and a black horse."

When night came, Jack went into the byre. The master came home. He asked where the boy was.

"I don't know where he is," said the mistress. "He came in here and sat down by the fire. I bade him bring in a cleeve of turf. He said he wouldn't. I said he shouldn't be there if he didn't work. He said he wouldn't do a turn till night. We had a quarrel. I haven't set eyes on him since then."

They went to bed. They heard a noise in the byre. "The cattle have broken loose," said the mistress. "They are goring one another." The master called to the servant-girl to go out and look into the byre ; that the cattle were broken loose. The girl got up and went out. She was a while outside. She couldn't catch the cattle. The master got up himself and went out. The girl was in the byre before him. He kissed the girl. They came in. The master said two of the cattle were broken loose. Jack was in the byre all the time watching them, and when they went to bed he came into the house and went to bed. He got up on the morrow morning. "I never saw the work I'd rather do than ploughing," said he. "It's time to turn the soil up. Let us go ploughing to-day."

"I don't care," said the master. They got the breakfast ready. They took the beasts with them to go ploughing. The two beasts were black. "I never saw anything I disliked more than a black beast." Jack went in and brought out a white sheet. He put it on one of the beasts. He then had a black beast and a white beast. They went ploughing the land that was nearest to them. When the middle of the day came, Jack raised his head, and he ploughing. He looked before him.

He saw the woman coming near them, with a bundle in her hand. "I don't know," said he, "who that woman over there is." The master looked.

"It is my wife," said he, "coming with our dinner.

"What a right sort of woman!" said Jack.

"When the mistress came to them she was ashamed to go past. They sat down and went to take their dinner. They had a good dinner. There were a great many eggs.

"It's a pity," said the master, "the man over there hasn't some dinner."

"Musha," said Jack, "I'll go and bring him some."

"Do," said the mistress.

Jack got up, and said he, "I'll take some eggs to be eating on the way." He took a handful of eggs. When he was gone a little way from them he let one of the eggs fall on the ground. He was dropping the eggs on the road. When he got as far as the man he sat down and began chatting.

Said the mistress, "He won't come over till the dinner's good for nothing."

"I'll go over myself," said the master. He got up and he went over, but he wasn't gone far when he came on an egg. He stooped and picked it up. He was gathering the eggs on the road.

"What's the man beyond gathering?" said the other man to Jack.

"He's gathering white stones to kill you for being with his wife yesterday in the lime-kiln."

"Did he hear of that?"

"He heard," said Jack.

"I'll stay here no longer," said the man.

He got up and went running away as fast as he could. The master began to call after him. He wouldn't turn back. The master kept running after him. When Jack saw the two of them travelling he went back to the dinner.

"Where is he gone to?" said the mistress.

"He's after that man for his doings with you in the lime-kiln yesterday."

The master came back to his dinner. When the mistress saw him coming she got up and took to her heels. When the master saw that, he asked where was she going?

"She's going to drown herself," said Jack, "for your kissing the servant girl in the byre last night."

"Did she hear of that?" said the master. He went running after her. "Come back," said he, "and I'll never do it again."

"Oh, don't kill me," said she, "and I'll never do it again."

She returned then and they took their dinner, but it was good for nothing. They ploughed till night-time. Jack was a good servant-boy. He put in his time.

When he left his master he went to the big town. He went tailoring. His master had twelve boys before he came. Jack wasn't long with him when he was a great hand at the sewing. His time was nearly up. His master thought he would keep no one but Jack. The times were hard. He dismissed them every one but Jack. He kept him. They were tailoring one day. The master said to Jack it was a bad year.

"Don't be afraid," said Jack. "Do you see that field full of cattle over there?"

When night came Jack and his master went out. They went to the field. Jack took one of the bullocks. He skinned the skin off it. He cut the flesh off the bones. He sewed the skin on the bullock again. They went home, and two loads of meat with them. They had enough that time. To make a long story short, they didn't leave a bullock in the field but they did the same to. When the last of the cattle was eaten, they began with the sheep. They played the same trick on the sheep.

When the king thought it was time to kill a bullock he went to the butcher. They went to the field. When they went to look at a bullock, the bullock was barely able to walk. They were all like that. The king couldn't tell what happened them. They went to the field where the sheep were. They were in bad condition. There wasn't a sheep or a head of cattle that Jack and the tailor hadn't eaten the flesh off.

The king went home, and he didn't know what to do. He went to the old man who was in the town to tell him what happened to them.

" There's some neighbour of yours that's smart."

" I don't know how I can get hold of him."

" I know," said the old man. " The first fine day that comes take some gold and silver, spread it out, and leave it outside till the dark comes. Whoever is playing the tricks on you will spy it. He'll try for it. When night comes, take in the money and put out a barrel of pitch."

The king did so. Jack looked out at the window. He saw the king spread out the money. " Do you see," said he, " what the man is doing yonder ? " Jack was watching the money all day. Night was coming on, and nobody was going near the money. " He has forgotten it," said Jack ; " no one will come near it till morning."

When night came Jack and his master went drawing near the money, to take home the full of a bag with them. They went to the place where the money was. There was a barrel of pitch there. " Which will you do, stoop into the barrel, or watch ? " The tailor said he would stoop. He stooped into the barrel ; he stretched his two hands down to get a handful. The two hands stuck in the pitch. He was caught then. He could not stir. He called to Jack to draw him out of the barrel. Jack went to draw him. He failed to draw him. He placed his two hands on his body and shoved him down on the crown of his head. He left him there.

The king came in the morning. He found the thief caught in the barrel. He couldn't tell then who he was, he was so black with pitch. He was as bad as ever. He went to the old man again. He said the thief was caught by him, but he didn't know who he was.

"Do you know what you'll do? Take a beast and tie him to the beast's tail. Whoever it is that has lost her husband, when she sees him she will go crying."

He tied a rope on the man. He put him behind the beast. He went through the big town with him. He did not go far till he came to the house of the tailor. When the tailor's wife saw him she gave a roar of lamentation out of her. Jack caught hold of the scissors and cut the tip of his finger. The king came in. He said she was caught. The tailor (*i.e.*, Jack) looked round. "What ails you?" said Jack.

"It is your wife who has lost the man and is crying there."

"It was I cut my finger," said Jack, " and she

8

thought I was killed, and that's what she was crying for. You may go off with yourself. There's
nothing for you to get here."

The king went away. He was up and he was
down. If he were to be walking till now he
wouldn't get one to go crying. He had nothing
for it but to go home. The tailor's wife and Jack
were married then.

THE SERVANT* OF POVERTY.

Narrator, P. MINAHAN, *Malinmore, Glencolumkille,
co. Donegal.*

THERE was a rich farmer there. He was
going from home to buy cattle The
king and the farmer met. Each of them got a
letter that there was a young son born to the
farmer, a young daughter to the king. They
were rejoiced when they heard it. They went both
into a tavern to drink a glass. They made it up
that if the children would agree to it they would
have them married. They went home then. They
were rejoiced at the children.

It was not long after that when the farmer died.
His wife was broken up. She had nothing but
the child. She had to sell the farm and the stock.
She was not worth a penny. She was bringing
up the child till he was fit to go to school. He
would be out on the street, and anyone who would
have anything to carry, the boy would carry it for

* Or "Spouse of Poverty."

him. They would give him sixpence or a shilling. He would give that to the master of the school, till the last of it was spent. He was coming on with his learning, till he was a good scholar. He was on the street one day. The king was there. The king bought a quarter of mutton. The king looked about him. He saw the little boy opposite watching him. He asked him would he carry it. The boy said he would carry. The king went with the boy. When they came to the house the king gave him half-a-crown. The boy went home rejoiced. He gave that to the master. He was at school till the half-crown was spent. One day the daughter of the king was on the street. She bought a parcel of clothes. She looked about her. The boy was behind her. She asked him would he carry the parcel. He said he would carry. The two went to the king's house. When the king saw the two coming in, he went laughing. The girl gave the boy another half-crown. She asked her father what was the reason of his laughing. Her father said there was none. The girl said there was no harm in it. The king said that at one time the boy was as good as herself. He told her everything that had passed, nor did she pretend anything. She had an eye on the boy from that out. She was giving him money to keep him at school, till he was a good scholar, till he was growing too big to be at school.

"What would you think of being a pedlar?" said she.

"I have no money," said the boy.

She gave him five pounds. He went to buy hardware. He met a fighting cock. He bet his five pounds on the cock. The cock was beaten, and his five pounds were lost on him. He went home then. She met him at the end of a couple of days.

"How did you get on?" said she.

"I met a fighting cock. I bet my five pounds on the cock. The cock was beaten. I lost the five pounds."

"Well! here are five other pounds," said the girl. "Do no foolishness with them, till you buy the hardware."

He went then. He fell in with a race-horse. He took a conceit on the horse. He bet the five pounds. The beast was beaten. The five pounds were lost. He had to go home. He was afraid to come across the girl. He was leaving the way for fear he should meet her. He met her one day.

"Well, how did you get on?" said she.

"I believe you will kill me," said he. "I lost the five pounds again."

"Well," said she, "unless there was venture in you, you would not have lost them. If you got five pounds more, I think you would not lose them."

"I would not," said he.

She gave him five pounds more. He went. He bought the five pounds' worth of hardware. He came home. He went pedlaring. He was doing well till he sold everything. He doubled his money. He came home then. She met him.

"You have made your way home," said she.

"I have made," said he.

"How did you get on ?" said she.

"Very well," said he. "I have doubled my money."

"Buy ten pounds' worth now," said she.

He bought the ten pounds' worth. He struck to pedlaring again, till he sold the ten pounds' worth. He came home then. She met him.

"You have got home," said she.

"I have got," said he.

"How did you succeed?" said she.

"Very well," said he ; "I have twenty pounds now."

"Good you are," said she. "Buy twenty pounds' worth now."

He was buying and selling, till his pack was so heavy that he was tired with it. He came home. She met him. He said he was growing tired carrying the pack. Would she give him leave to buy a beast to carry it ? She said she would give him leave. He went to buy a beast. He was buying and selling then till he had a great

deal of money. He came home then. She came
to him. He asked her would she give him leave
to set up a shop in the town. He was afraid he
would be killed for his money. She said she
would give him leave. He set up a shop then
and he laid in a stock. He was selling as much
as any two in the city.

The king was dealing with a merchant from
London. He came to Dublin to settle with the
king. They went to settle. They could not
agree. They got a couple of clerks to settle
between them. The clerks could not settle it all.
They were three days sitting at the settling.
They failed. The king came home at night.
His daughter came to him.

"How are you and the London man getting
on?"

"They have failed to settle it," said the king.

"Did you try the shopman?" said she. "They
say he has good learning."

"We did not try," said he.

"Try him to-morrow," said she.

He went on the morning of the morrow. They
sat down to the settling again. They sent word
for the shopman. He came. He began to look
into the books. He made it up in a moment
between the king and the man from London.
The king was satisfied then. He went home.
His daughter asked him how he got on. The

king said he got on very well, that he never saw
a better scholar. The London man came to the
young man the next day, to find out how much
he would take for a year. The young man said
he could not leave his shop. The London man
said he would give him more than he would make
by his shop in a year. He made advice to go
with him. He went home. He went to find out
if she would give him leave. She said she would
give. He put his shop to auction. He sold it
out. He made ready to go with the man from
London. He went with him then. He was
sending letters to her. She was reading them.
When the year was up, he was making ready to
go home. The London man said to him to stay
another year. He made advice to stay. He
remained another year. When the year was up
he made ready to go. He filled a ship full of
every kind of goods. He bade the captain go to
Dublin in the name of Kayleh-na-Bochtjinacht.
When the captain came to Dublin there was no
one at all of that name to be found. He did not
know what to do. He had nothing for it but to
return home. He was angry. The king was in
the city. He went to tell at home that there was a
ship was come from London with a cargo of goods,
in the name of Kayleh-na-Bochtjinacht, and that
there was no one at all in the place of that name.

"Well," said the king's daughter, "the cargo

will go to loss. Prepare a store of your own, and empty the cargo into it. Perhaps the owner will come to look for it."

The king got men, and they unloaded the cargo into the store. The captain was rejoiced when he got the vessel unloaded. When two years were up with Kayleh-na-Bochtjinacht he was coming home. He was walking round by the foot of the sea. A collegian met him, going the same road. He asked Kayleh-na-Bochtjinacht where he was going. Kayleh answered he did not know well where he was going; that he made a herring-net, and the first night he put it out he had not seen it since; that he was walking round by the foot of the sea to look if he could find it rolled on to a stone.

" Where are you going yourself ? "

" I am going to Dublin, to be married to the daughter of the king."

" Well, I will be with you a bit of the way."

A rainy day came on them, and they were greatly wet. This young man, he was all but perished with cold.

" If you had your own house from the town with you, you would not be wet."

They went on till they came to a river. There was no bridge at all on the river. Kayleh-na-Bochtjinacht went out into the river. He went across. The young champion went out after him

till he was all but lost. When he got to the other
side of the river, "I was all but lost," said he.

"Well, if you had your own bridge with you,
you would not be lost."

They went on another while. The champion
said he was hungry. Kayleh said, "If you had
your mother with you from home, you would not
be hungry."

Kayleh had a loaf with him. He drew it out
and took his dinner. They went on then till they
came to Dublin. Kayleh stopped at the end of
the town. The young champion went to the
king's house. He was all but famished. He
went into the parlour then. They took their
dinner. They were passing fun. The young
woman was with them.

"Well," said the young champion, "there was
a fine man with me to-day, he had the silliest talk
ever I heard. When I met him, I asked him how
far he was going. He said he did not well know;
that he made a herring-net; the first night he put
it out into the sea he never had a sight of it since;
that he was walking by the foot of the sea, to look
if he would fall in with it in a creek, or rolled on
a rock. We went on another while. A day of
rain came. We were wet greatly. I called out
that I was wet.

" 'Well,' said the man, 'if you had your house
with you, you would not be wet.'

"We went on another while, till we came to a river. There was a great flood in the river. The man went out. He went to the other side. I went out after him, so that I was all but lost. I said I was all but lost. 'If you had your bridge with you, you would have had no fear of being lost.' We went on another while. I said I was hungry. 'Well,' said the man, 'if you had your mother with you from home, you would not have been hungry.'" The king was listening to him.

"Well," said he, "when you called out that you were wet, that man had a top-coat on, that didn't let a drop in. When you called out you were all but lost on the river, if you had a nag you would not have been afraid. The other man had a good horse."

"He had," said the champion.

"As good as I ever saw," said the king's daughter.

"How far was he with you?"

"He was with me to the end of the city."

She arose standing. She went out, nor did she stop till she was in the city, in the place where was Kayleh-na-Bochtjinacht. She took a hold of him by the hand. She bade him welcome home. He got up and opened a travelling bag. He gave her a silk gown. He put it on her. He put silk clothes entirely on her. The two went till they came to the king's house. The king and the champion thought the bride was in a room inside.

There was a knock at the door. The housemaid arose and opened it. The young couple came in. They asked the maid if the priest was in the king's house. She said he was ; that the champion and the king's daughter were to be married. " I would like to see the king," said Kayleh. The maid went to the king. She told him there was a gentleman to see the wedding. The king arose. He opened the parlour door. Kayleh came to him. He said he was a stranger, that he had a woman with him to get married to ; he would be thankful to the king to get the first chance of being married. The king said he would give it to him and welcome. The young couple went into the room where the priest was. They were married. They came out and they married. The bride came forward to the king and the champion. She took hold of the young champion by the shoulder. She told him to go home to his mother—"The silly man that was with you to-day, I am married to him now." " You thought you were wise," said the king ; " but it is you were the fool, not that man." He had nothing for it then but to get up and go home. The king's daughter then told her father who the husband was she had. There was great joy on the king then that the lad got on so well.

They built a big house then in the city. When it was ready, they put into it the goods that were

in the store. The master that was in London
came into the harbour with his ship. When
Kayleh heard he was there he was rejoiced. He
went out to see him. The captain was rejoiced
to see him. Kayleh went praising his wife. "You
are a fool," said the captain; "maybe she's the
worst in the world." "How much will you wager
on it? I'll lay my shop against your ship that
you won't find her yielding."

They laid the wager. The captain was going
out then. "What proof shall I bring that I have
had my way with her." "There is a gold ring
on her finger. Have that for me." "Stay you
here," said the captain, "till I come."

The captain went on shore. He went to her.
She was rejoiced to see him. She said to herself
that the captain was taking liberties with her. She
went into a room. She locked the door and left
his sight. The captain did not know then what
to do. He was afraid his ship was lost. He
went to the kitchen to the maid. He drew out
a purse of money. He said he would give her
the purse if she would open the door of the room.
She covered the money. She took the lock off the
door. The captain went to the woman. He said
he would not leave the room till she drank a drop
of his whiskey. To get rid of him she drank a
drop of the whiskey. What was in it but a sleeping drop! She fell asleep. The captain took the

ring from her finger. He went to Kayleh. When Kayleh saw he had the ring, the shop was lost. He went home. When the woman saw she had lost the ring, she knew it was all over with her. She went away. He was raging with anger. If he got hold of her he would kill her. She went away ashamed. The captain went to live in the house. He was selling the goods. Kayleh went off wandering. She went and put a man's clothes on her. She went to a city. She went to a tailor's shop. She asked the tailor if he wanted a young man. The tailor said he would not mind taking one. She made it up with him. She would sell as much as three. He thought it was a man was with him. He was with him for a year. A poor man came to the city selling brooms. He spent a couple of days in the city. The mob was casting it up to that tailor that a man from his country was selling brooms. She said there was never a man from her country who sold brooms. She rose out one evening. She went through the city to try if she could find him. She met him, and he with a load of brooms. She asked him if that was his means of living. The poor man said it was—that he was all that day, and few were the brooms he sold. She asked him how much he got for them apiece. He said he got only a halfpenny. She put her hand in her pocket and gave him the price of his load.

" Throw them away from you. Have you any learning at all? " said she.

" I have a trifle," said the poor man.

" Do you think you could do as a clerk in a shop? "

" I think I could do."

The tailor went and bought a suit of clothes for him. She put them on him. He and the tailor went to the shop.

"Here's a young man I have got for you," said she.

He hired the young man for a year. The young man came to him and was serving him well. Better was the learning that he had than the shopman's. The tailor was content as they were together. They were the two comrades; nor did he ever recognise the tailor. They were a couple of years in the city. One day the tailor said they were there long enough, and would go home for a while now. He said he would never go home. She said she would, that they would get a place as good as to be there. They got ready and were drawing towards Dublin. The clerk said he would not go near the city. She said she would go. They walked on till they came to the city. There was no going through the street for the clerk. He became sorrowful and troubled. They were walking till they came to the house they used to live in.

" This is a good house," said the tailor ; " we'll go in to see if they will keep us for the night."

" We will not go into that house on any account."

" We'll go to no other place but that," said the tailor.

They went in and got place till morning. The captain was living there always. There were gentlemen dining with him. The tailor was making fun for the girls in the kitchen. He began dancing and singing. The clerk was sitting under the window, with his head bent down. When the gentlemen heard the singing and the dancing in the kitchen, they opened the parlour door to see the tailor playing his music. They bade him come up to the parlour, to themselves. He said he would like to have his companion with him. They bade the two come. The two went up. They got whiskey. They made the tailor sing. He was performing a while. He looked about him.

" This is a fine house you have," said he. " I have travelled far enough, but I never in my travellings met with a better house than this of yours."

" Simply I got this house." He told the gentlemen how he came into the house.

" Well," said the tailor, " you bear witness to everything you have heard. I was the woman, that was in the house, to whom that happened."

She opened her bosom to show it was a woman.

"Get up, you gillie over there." She locked the parlour door. Kayleh went for the police. The police came. They arrested the captain. The gentlemen were witnesses. The captain was put in prison. She put off the tailor's clothes then. They arrested the maid and put her in prison. They fell into their house and place again. They were then as they were ever. The report went out through the city that Kayleh and the king's daughter were in their own house again. The king then made a dinner and invited them to it. They were eating and drinking for three nights and three days.

SIMON AND MARGARET.

Narrator, Michael Faherty, *Renvyle, co. Galway.*

LONG ago there was a king's son called Simon, and he came in a ship from the east to Eire. In the place where he came to harbour he met with a woman whose name was Margaret, and she fell in love with him. And she asked him if he would take her with him in the ship. He said he would not take her, that he had no business with her, " for I am married already," said he. But the day he was going to sea she followed him to the ship, and such a beautiful woman was she that he said to himself that he would not put her out of the ship; " but before I go farther I must get beef." He returned back and got the beef. He took the woman and the beef in the ship, and he ordered the sailors to make everything ready that they might be sailing on the sea. They were not long from land when they saw a great bulk making towards them, and it seemed to them it was more like a serpent than anything else whatever. And it was not long till the serpent cried out, "Throw me the Irish person you have on board."

"We have no Irish person in the ship," said the king's son, "for it is foreign people we are; but we have meat we took from Eire, and, if you wish, we will give you that."

"Give it to me," said the serpent, "and everything else you took from Eire."

He threw out a quarter of the beef, and the serpent went away that day, and on the morrow morning she came again, and they threw out another quarter, and one every day till the meat was gone. And the next day the serpent came again and she cried out to the king's son, "Throw the Irish flesh out to me."

"I have no more flesh," said the prince.

"If you have not flesh, you have an Irish person," said the serpent, "and don't be telling your lies to me any longer. I knew from the beginning that you had an Irish person in the ship, and unless you throw her out to me, and quickly, I will eat yourself and your men."

Margaret came up, and no sooner did the serpent see her than she opened her mouth, and put on an appearance as if she were going to swallow the ship.

"I will not be guilty of the death of you all," said Margaret; "get me a boat, and if I go far safe it is better; and if I do not go, I had rather I perished than the whole of us."

" What shall we do to save you ? " said Simon.

" You can do nothing better than put me in the boat," said she, " and lower me on the sea, and leave me to the will of God."

As soon as she got on the sea, no sooner did the serpent see her than she desired to swallow her, but before she reached as far as her, a billow of the sea rose between them, and left herself and the boat on dry land. She saw not a house in sight she could go to. " Now," said she, " I am as unfortunate as ever I was. There is no place at all for me to get that I know of, and this is no place for me to be." She arose and she began to walk, and after a long while she saw a house a good way from her. " I am not as unfortunate as I thought," said she. " Perhaps I shall get lodging in that house to-night." She went in, and there was no one in it but an old woman, who was getting her supper ready. " I am asking for lodging till morning."

" I will give you no lodging," said the old woman.

" Before I go farther, there is a boat there below, and it is better for you to take it into your hands."

" Come in," said the old woman, " and I will give you lodging for the night."

The old woman was always praying by night and day. Margaret asked her, "Why are you always saying your prayers?"

"I and my mother were living a long while ago in the place they call the White Doon, and a giant came and killed my mother, and I had to come away for fear he would kill myself; and I am praying every night and every day that some one may come and kill the giant."

The next morning there came a gentleman and a beautiful woman into the house, and he gave the old woman the full of a quart of money to say paters for them till morning. The old woman opened a chest and took out a handsome ring, and tried to place it on his finger, but it would not go on. "Perhaps it would fit you," said she to the lady. But her finger was too big.

When they went out Margaret asked the old woman who were the man and woman. "That is the son of a king of the Eastern World, and the name that is on him is Stephen, and he and the woman are going to the White Doon to fight the giant, and I am afraid they will never come back; for the ring did not fit either of them; and it was told to the people that no one would kill the giant but he whom the ring would fit."

The two of them remained during the night praying for him, for fear the giant should kill him; and early in the morning they went out to see what had happened to Stephen and the lady that was with him, and they found them dead near the White Doon.

"I knew," said the old woman, "this is what what would happen to them. It is better for us to take them with us and bury them in the churchyard." When they were buried, "Come home," said the old woman, "and we'll know who is the first person comes the same way again."

About a month after a man came into the house, and no sooner was he inside the door than Margaret recognised him.

"How have you been ever since, Simon?"

"I am very well," said he; "it can't be that you are Margaret?"

"It is I," said she.

"I thought that billow that rose after you, when you got into the boat, drowned you."

"It only left me on dry land," said Margaret.

"I went to the Eastern World, and my father said to me that he sent my brother to go and fight with the giant, who was doing great damage to the people near the White Doon, and that my wife went to carry his sword."

"If that was your brother and your wife," said Margaret, "the giant killed them."

"I will go on the spot and kill the giant, if I am able."

"Wait till I try the ring on your finger," said the old woman.

"It is too small to go on my finger," said he.

"It will go on mine," said Margaret.

"It will fit you," said the old woman.

Simon gave the full of a quart of money to the old woman, that she might pray for him till he came back. When he was about to go, Margaret said, "Will you let me go with you?"

"I will not," said Simon, "for I don't know that the giant won't kill myself, and I think it too much that one of us should be in this danger."

"I don't care," said Margaret. "In the place where you die, there am I content to die."

"Come with me," said he.

When they were on the way to the White Doon, a man came before them.

"Do you see that house near the castle?" said the man.

"I see," said Simon.

"You must go into it and keep a candle lighted till morning in it."

"Where is the giant?" said Simon.

"He will come to fight you there," said the man.

They went in and kindled a light, and they were not long there when Margaret said to Simon,—

"Come, and let us see the giants."

"I cannot," said the king, "for the light will go out if I leave the house."

"It will not go out," said Margaret; "I will keep it lighted till we come back."

And they went together and got into the castle, to the giant's house, and they saw no one there but an old woman cooking; and it was not long till she opened an iron chest and took out the young giants and gave them boiled blood to eat.

"Come," said Margaret, "and let us go to the house we left."

They were not long in it when the king's son was falling asleep.

Margaret said to him, "If you fall asleep, it will not be long till the giants come and kill us."

"I cannot help it," he said. "I am falling asleep in spite of me."

He fell asleep, and it was not long till Margaret heard a noise approaching, and the giant cried from outside to the king's son to come out to him.

"Fum, faw, faysogue! I feel the smell of a lying churl of an Irishman. You are too great for one bite and too little for two, and I don't know whether it is better for me to send you into the Eastern World with a breath or put you under my feet in the puddle. Which would you rather have—striking with knives in your ribs or fighting on the grey stones?"

"Great, dirty giant, not with right or rule did I come in, but by rule and by right to cut your head off in spite of you, when my fine, silken feet go up and your big, dirty feet go down."

They wrestled till they brought the wells of fresh water up through the grey stones with fighting and breaking of bones, till the night was all but gone. Margaret squeezed him, and the first squeeze she put him down to his knees, the second squeeze to his waist, and the third squeeze to his armpits.

"You are the best woman I have ever met. I will give you my court and my sword of light and the half of my estate for my life, and spare to slay me."

"Where shall I try your sword of light?"

"Try it on the ugliest block in the wood."

"I see no block at all that is uglier than your own great block."

She struck him at the joining of the head and the neck, and cut the head off him.

In the morning when she wakened the king's son, "Was not that a good proof I gave of myself last night?" said he to Margaret. "That is the head outside, and we shall try to bring it home."

He went out, and was not able to stir it from the ground. He went in and told Margaret he could not take it with him, that there was a pound's weight in the head. She went out and took the head with her.

"Come with me," said he.

"Where are you going?"

"I will go to the Eastern World; and come with me till you see the place."

When they got home Simon took Margaret with him to his father the king.

"What has happened to your brother and your wife?" said the king.

"They have both been killed by the giants. And it is Margaret, this woman here, who has killed them."

The king gave Margaret a hundred thousand welcomes, and she and Simon were married,* and how they are since then I do not know.

* Simon's wife, mentioned at the beginning of the story, has apparently been forgotten.

THE SON OF THE KING OF PRUSSIA.

Narrator, P. M'GRALE, *Achill, co. Mayo.*

THERE were giants at that time, and every seven years three daughters of kings were left to them to be eaten, unless some one were found to fight them. In this year the kings came together, and they cast lots to see which of them should give his children to the giants to be eaten. And the lot fell on the High King of Erin to give his three daughters to the giants. Then came the son of the King of Prussia to ask the king's daughter in marriage, and the king said he could not give her to him unless he would fight the giants, and he said he would fight if he got good feeding.

And the king asked him, " What sort of food would you like best ? "

Said he, " Marrow of deer and sinews of beeves." And the king said he would give him that.

There were servants killing for him his sufficiency of food, and he rose out, the son of the

King of Prussia, and he went among the work-people, and when he would strike one of them a blow of his fist and kill him the king would not say anything for fear of making him angry. Then, when he came within a month of the time, he went to the glen, and tools with him to make a hole in the glen, and he was at home every evening, and he dirty.

When it came within a week of the time, the son of the King of Scotland spoke to his father. Said he, " A good neighbour to you was the King of Erin ever."

" Good he was, my son, and I to him likewise."

" And he never put war nor battle on you."

" Nor I on him, my son."

" I am making one request of you, father."

" Every request you make of me I will give you, except to go to fight in Erin."

" Won't you give me that, father ? "

" I have fear of your getting married."

" My hand and my word to you, father, that that woman I will not wed till I come back to you."

" With that request, go, and I will give you my blessing."

He went with himself, then, and he arrayed himself in his clothes, and the stars of the son of a king by a queen were on the breast of his coat, and a poor man's suit outside, till he came to the sea, and took a great ship, till he came to Erin, and drew up his ship on the land, and put on her fastening for a day and a year, though he might chance to be there but an hour.

He went then to the house of the hen-wife, and asked for lodging; and he got lodging for the night; and the old woman asked him what was the news, and he said he had no news at all unless he would get it from her.

" I'd say," said she, " that it was under a docking you came out, when you've heard nothing of the great gathering that's to be here to-morrow. There are three giants to come, on three days, one after the other, and they are to get the three daughters of the King of Erin, and the son of the King of Prussia, is to fight for them; and, if he kills the giants, the first person to-morrow that brings the news the giant's head is cut off, will get a shovel of gold."

Then the poor man and the hen-wife spent the night pleasantly, and in the morning he got up and washed his hands and his face, and ate his breakfast, and went to the glen, and he sat down in a clump of ferns, brambles, and nettles, and there was he.

Then the king and his people went drawing to the glen, and when they were near it the son of the King of Prussia told them to go home, for fear the giant might come and kill some of them before he could stop him. The king and his people

went home and left the son of the King of Prussia
and the young girl in the glen, and she sat down
on a stone chair, and the son of the King of
Prussia was coming about her, thinking to make
free with her, till he ran to his hole and left
her there.

Then he saw the ship coming under sail, three
lengths before she came near to land, and the giant
cast anchor, and gave a step on the land, and he
all but sank the ship after him; and the land, when
he came on it, shook so greatly that the old castles
fell, and the castles that were made last stooped;
every (old) tree was broken, and the young tree
was bent; and he left not foal with mare, nor calf
with cow, nor lamb with sheep, nor hare in a bush,
nor rabbit in hole, that didn't go off in terror.
And he came up to the girl and put the tip of his
finger under the edge of her girdle, and threw her
over the tip of his shoulder.

" My mischief and misfortune! Hadn't your
father a man, cow-boy nor sheep-boy, to-day to
fight me? Or where is the son of the King of
Prussia, who has been feeding for a year to fight
me? Don't think it's on feather beds I'll put
you, nor up the stairs, when I bring you home;
but you are big for one bite and small for two,
and if I had a grain of salt I would eat you at one
bite; and small is the morsel you are between
myself and my two brothers."

He went with her, drawing to the ship to get on board; and the son of the King of Scotland spoke to him, and said he should not get her like that without fighting. And the giant said that it wasn't worth his while to let her out of his hands, but for him to come and prevent him taking her with him. But the other man said that was not right, that he should put the woman down on the land, and fight honourably. And then the giant asked him which he liked best, wrestling on the red flagstones, or green knives at the top of his ribs. He said that he liked best wrestling on the red flagstones, in the place where his noble white feet should be rising above the giant's clumsy club feet. The two champions caught hold of each other in the grip of the close, keen wrestling. If you were to go seeking for sport from the west of the world to the world's beginning, it is to that pair you would go. They made soft of the hard, and hard of the soft, till they drew the springs of fresh water under the red stones; till the son of the King of Scotland remembered that he came there without the King of Erin knowing, nor his daughters, that he was come; and also that his father was not pleased with his coming; and he gave the giant a squeeze, and put him down to his two knees in the ground, and the second squeeze to the waist of his trousers, and the third squeeze to the back of his neck.

" A green sod over you, churl ! "

" Stay, stay ! best of champions that ever I saw.
I am but a third of the world, and my brother is
the half of the world, and the other is as strong
as the world ; and if you spare me, I and my
brothers will be your helpers, and we will conquer
the world."

" That's not what I will do," said the son of
the King of Scotland; " but I will cut the head
off you."

And he caught hold of his sword and cut the
head off the giant. And the young girl all the
time was watching the young champion ; and she
ran to him and kissed him, and asked him if he
would come home with her, and he said he would
not come. She took a pair of scissors and cut
away a piece of the champion's suit that was
on him.

He went with himself then, and came to the
hen-wife, and told her that the giant's head was cut
off; and she asked him if any one was before her
to the king with the news. And she ran to the
king and told him the giant's head was cut off,
and he gave her a shovel of gold as the reward of
her trouble.

When the son of the King of Scotland was gone,
the son of the King of Prussia arose out of his
hole, and he took with him a book and a knife,
and he swore that unless she said it was he had

done the action, he would cut the head off her father and every one of them. He took his sword and he cut a piece from the giant's head, and took it home in proof that he killed the giant.

The king came and his hosts before him, and they raised him on their shoulders and carried him home. And there was great joy on the king and his people that the giant was killed; and the two other sisters were cheerful; but there was dissatisfaction and sorrow and trouble on the third sister, and she spoke not a word to them except to say, "You will have it yet."

The king spent the night cheerfully, till the whiteness of the day came upon the morrow.

The next day the second sister went out, and the son of the King of Scotland fought for her, and when he would not go home with her, she cut off a lock of his hair; but the son of the King of Prussia said it was he killed the giant. And the next day the third sister went out, and the son of the King of Scotland killed the third giant. The girl asked him would he go home with her, and he said he would not, and she took with her one of his shoes.

And when the son of the King of Prussia went home, and the third giant killed by the son of the King of Scotland, proclamation was made of the marriage of the son of the King of Prussia, and the daughter of the King of Erin. And when

10

they ate their supper, word was sent to the priest
of the pattens and the clerk of the table, (to come)
to marry them. And the hen-wife came and the
champion to the wedding ; and they arose that
the pair might be married. The priest asked the
girl if she would marry that man, and she said she
would not. And he struck her a box with his
fist, and said, " How do you know that you are
my choice ? Haven't I my choice of the family
to get ? " And the king said he had.

Then came the second daughter, and the priest
asked her, would she marry him ? and she said
she would not. And he struck her a blow of his
fist, and he said, " How do you know that you are
my choice ? Haven't I my choice of you to get ? "
And the king said he had.

Then came the third girl, and the priest asked
her, would she marry him ? and she said she would
not. And the son of the King of Prussia gave
her a blow of his fist, and he said, " How do you
know that you are my choice ? Haven't I my
choice of you to get ? " And the king said he
had.

Then the Scotchman got up and he gave the
son of the King of Prussia a blow with the tip of
his boot and knocked him down. And the king
offered a reward of five pounds to whoever would
tell who struck the champion. And, as there
were bad people present, he was told it was the

old man down there who had struck him. He was caught, and he was bound, and when the daughters saw him they knew him, and they threw themselves on their knees before their father and begged he would grant them one request; and he said he would, but that one of them must marry the man.

"It is not for that man we are asking, but for this one, who saved us."

He put the three daughters in three rooms, and he called the eldest, and she came to him and told him that he was the man who saved her. She put her hand in her pocket and she took out the piece she cut from his champion's suit, and it answered to the coat. Then the king called the second daughter, and she said likewise, and showed the lock of hair, and her father was satisfied. He called the third daughter, and she showed the shoe, and she said she had no fear of him, that he it was who saved her.

The Scotchman got up standing, and he bound the son of the King of Prussia, and they were going to put him to death. Then the daughters asked the son of the King of Scotland if he would marry any of them, and he said that to one of them he was bound; but that when he knew what the son of the King of Prussia was going to do he came without* his father's leave to Erin to

* This contradicts what is stated on page 140.

save them, "and I cannot marry a woman till I go to my father and then I will come back to you."

And the daughter said, "Marry one of us and then go to your father, and then you can come back."

He said he could not do that, that he would go to his father first. Said she,—

"If you do not marry one of us, I will put you for a year under disesteem and bad esteem ; every one will be spitting on you and cursing you ; who-ever is meanest you shall be under his curses ; and till you marry one of us, or get cause for laughter, your mouth to be at the back of your head."

And when he saw that, "If I were going this hour to marry you, I would not marry you now."

The disfigurement came on him. He turned to the door and opened his hand, and all that were between him and the door he killed. He went on from place to place in hopes of getting a cure for himself, and he left not a doctor in the place that he was not getting the water of healing and every sort of drugs from them.

He was going till a man met him who was giving food and work to every one, and he went to him and asked him for work. The man said he would give it if the workmen would take him. He had eighteen men, six of them each in dif-ferent places he had, and he went up to one set of six and said to them, "Here is a helper I am bringing you; I don't think he'll increase our work, and I myself will give him enough to eat."

They spat upon him and said they would not have him.

Then they came to another six, and they would not take him; and they came to another, and they took him. And when the master went away, Crooked-mouth said he was sleepy, and asked for leave to sleep that day. And they gave him leave; and in the night he told them not to go out to work in the morning until he came in to his breakfast, and when he came in to his breakfast the work of a week was done. And those six were walking about and not doing a turn.

At that time a gentleman sent an invitation to dinner to the man (who had the workmen) and for his men to come with him. And they went drawing that way, and a robber met them on the road and bound every one of them and took his money from the master. And he told his men to bind Crooked-mouth, and Crooked-mouth said that not one should bind him but the robber himself.

"Come up to me and I'll bind you. You won't be having your stories to make of me."

When he went to bind him, Crooked-mouth laid hold of him, and turned him round, and threw him on the ground, and told him to hand out his master's money quickly, or he would kill him. So he gave him the money back and loosed the men.

"Master," said he, "here are twelve others for him, and I will do their work."

"Oh!" said the master, "I will not ask one turn of you, except one meal and one drink for ever."

So he gave over to the robber the twelve other men, who had refused to let him work with them. And before he parted with the robber he put him under obligations.

"I will not kill you," said he, "this is O'Daly, and I am Gerald O'Daly, and anything at all that's ever asked of you by the honour of O'Daly, do that."

Then they went on with themselves to the house, and there was a feast ready for them; and they took their meal, and while they were eating, the twelve others he gave over to the robber came. One of them asked the robber to let them go their way by the honour of O'Daly, and he told them to go and a hundred welcomes, and if it were a greater thing (he would grant it).

When Crooked-mouth ate his supper, he stretched himself under the table, and when the others ate their supper, (the gentleman) put them out to sleep in the barn, and when he came in he heard snoring, and he gave the man a kick, and asked him why he wasn't with the others, and he said he would not leave the house that night; and the man of the house said that he must leave; that no one slept in the house for a year, and that he should not sleep in it that night. But the other said he would sleep in it, and find out about everything in the house. He took the man of the house and put him in a basket, and put him in the chimney to smother him; and he asked him, "Let me down, and I will tell you." He let him down, but he would not tell him; and he put him back three times one after another, and the third time he came down he told him.

"I was one day standing at the gable of my house, and I saw a ship coming under full sail into the harbour, and a man and a woman jumped out (on the shore) and ran; and I saw a great monster in the sea coming the same way, and the monster ran after them; and the man put his hand in his pocket, and pulled out something, and flung it at the monster; and the monster sent out such a spout of blood that the two were drowned in it. I took them with me and washed them, and I put herbs of the hill on them, and I have had them for two years, and there is not a night since that I don't burn a penny candle looking at their beauty."

He opened a room and showed them to Crooked-mouth, and he took the water of healing and sprinkled some of it on them, and they arose alive again. And his mouth came as it was at first, and the disfigurement went from him, and he asked his brother what it was took him that way. And his brother said,—

" When you were gone a day and a year I went
to the sea, hoping to see a ship or boat that would
give me tidings of you, or to see if I would see
a board that I would recognise; and one day I
met a pretty bird-serpent, and a stone with him,
and it was written on the stone that that was the
stone that would kill the bird; and I took the
stone and the bird home with me, and I put
the bird into a cage, and kept it there for a week,
and it became so big I had to put it into the
stable; and it went on growing bigger and bigger
till I had to make a place for it in the wood, and
to tie the brambles round it, and I had four men
killing beef and giving it food. And one day I
was walking round near it, and it made a lunge at
me to eat me, and I said it would do that at last.
I went and took a ship, and went to sea, and I was
sailing three days when my sister rose up to me,
and I did not know she was on board the ship.
We were sailing till we came to the harbour, and
the serpent was following us, and I went up on the
land, and the serpent followed; and, as God was
helping me, I had my waistcoat on that day, and
the stone was in the pocket, and I flung the stone
at her, and she spouted so much blood that I
and my sister were drowned. I don't know what
happened to us since then."

" I took you with me, and cleansed you, and
put herbs of the hill round about you, and there

is not a night for two years I don't burn a penny candle looking on you, and I believe that it is I should get her in marriage."

The four spent the night pleasantly, telling one another everything; and in the morning when they arose, and the people who were at supper the night before were gathered together, the master did not recognise that Crooked-mouth was with him. But when Crooked-mouth told him that it was he was there, O'Daly bade him come with him, but he would not. He went with his brother and his sister and the other man to Scotland. And when they came to his father's court, his father was banished by Faugauns and Blue-men; and he and the other people who were taking possession of his father's court began; and he and they spent three nights and three days killing one another, and on the third day he had killed and banished them all. But when he and the cat met, the cat killed him and he killed the cat; and his brother was going everywhere that he killed, and at last he found him and the cat dead. And he searched his pocket and found in it the bottle of healing-water, and as he was drawing the cork from the bottle, some of the water fell on the dead man, and he arose alive again.

He went then with his sister and the other man who was in the place of husband to his sister; and they cleansed the king's castle, and he brought his father and mother and their people home to the castle, and they were well from that out. Then he gave his sister in marriage to the man, who found himself and her on the day when the serpent drowned them. There came the priest of the pattens and the clerk of the table, and the pair were wedded.

He himself then went back to Erin, and married the daughter of the King of Erin, who was to be eaten by the giants, and the son of the King of Prussia was to save her.

BEAUTY OF THE WORLD.

Narrator, P. MINAHAN, *Malinmore, Glencolumkille,*
co. Donegal.

THERE was a king then, and he had but one
son. He was out hunting. He was going
past the churchyard. There were four men in the
churchyard and a corpse. There was debt on the
corpse. The king's son went in. He asked what
was the matter, Said one of the men :

"The dead man is in our debt. I am not
willing to bury the body, till the two sons who
are here, promise to pay the debts."

"We are not able to pay," said one of them.

"I have five pounds," said the king's son ; "I
will give them to you to bury the body."

He gave the five pounds. The body was
buried. The king's son went hunting. He went
home in the evening. In the morning of the
morrow there was snow. He went out hunting
in the snow. He killed a black raven. He stood
over it and looked at it. He said in his own

mind he would never marry a woman whose head was not as black as the bird's wing, and her skin as white as the snow, and her cheeks as red as the blood on the snow.

He went home. On the morning of the morrow, when he rose, he washed himself, and he went away to find the woman. When he was going for a time, he met with a red-haired young man. The young man saluted him. He asked him where he was going. The king's son told him he was going to get one sight of that woman.

" It is better for you to hire me," said the young man.

" What wages do you be asking ? "

" Half of all we gain, to the end of a year and a day."

The two went on with themselves till the evening came. Said the red man :

" There is a man related to me living in this wood below. Do you wait here till I go down to him."

The red man went down to the house of the giant. The giant was sitting on a chair by the fire.

" Uncle, dear," said the red man, " is it like this you are ? "

" Yes, kinsman mine : what is coming to me ? "

Said the red man : " The King of the prodigious Eastern World is coming up to kill you. Get out of the way as quick as you can."

"I have an iron house outside there. Lock me into it."

He locked the man in. He went to his master. He took his master up to the house of the giant. He got ready their supper. They went to rest. This was the giant's cry in the morning. "Let them open." The red man went to him. He asked him what was the matter.

"I am ready to perish with hunger. Let me out of this quickly."

"I will not let you out," said the red man, "till you tell me where the dark cloak is."

"That is what I will never tell any one."

"Well, if you like better not to tell, you will be there till you die."

"Sooner than be here any longer, it is hanging in such a room."

"I know where it is," said the red man. "Be here as long as you like."

When the giant heard that he would not get out, he took a jump out between two bars of the iron house. Two halves were made of him. Half fell outside and half inside. The red man went to the giant's house. He got ready the breakfast. He and his master breakfasted. He took with them plenty of gold and silver, two horses and two saddles. They went till evening was there, and they went into another wood.

"I have an uncle," said the red man, "living

here. We shall get lodging to-night. Stay you here, till I go up."

The red men went in to the giant's house.

" Uncle, dear, is it here you are resting ? "

" Yes, kinsman, dear : what is coming on me ? "

" The King of the prodigious East is coming to kill you. Hide yourself as quick as you can."

" I have an iron house here outside. Lock me into it."

He locked him in. He brought his master. They made ready their supper. This was the giant's cry in the morning, " Let them open."

" I will not open," said the red man, " till you tell me where are the slippery shoes."

" They are under the bed."

" I know myself where they are," said the red man. " Stop there as long as you like."

When the giant saw he was not to get out, he took a leap between two bars of the iron house. Two halves were made of him. Half fell inside, and half out.

The red man and his master went on travelling till evening. They came to another wood. There was a giant in the wood. The red man did to him as to the other giants. He took from him the sword of light, and plenty of gold and silver.

" Now," said the red man to his master, " we shall be going home. We have got enough : go forward no farther. The woman you are approaching,—there is not a tree in the wood on which a man's head is not hung, except one tree that is waiting for your head. We'll return home."

"I will never go home," said the king's son, "till I get one sight of that woman."

They went forward till they came to the king's house. The king made great welcome for them. They took their dinner. They spent the night in drinking and sport. When they were sitting to their supper she came down from the top of the house. Her head was as black as the bird's wing, her skin as white as the snow, and her cheeks as red as the blood. She came to them, to the place where they were eating. She threw him a comb. Said she, "If you have not that comb to give me to-morrow, I will cut your head from you."

He took hold of the comb. He put it down in his pocket. When they were going to bed the red man said, "See if you have the comb." He put his fingers in his pocket. He had not the comb. His tears fell.

"It's a pity I did not take your advice when you told me to return home."

"Perhaps we shall get the better of her entirely," said the red man. He was comforting him till he got him to bed. When he got him to bed he put on the dark cloak. He took with him

the slippery shoes and the sword of light.   He
went out and stood in the back yard.   She came
out.   She made down to the sea.   She came to
the sea.   She threw a shell from her pocket.
She made a boat of it.   She went into the boat.
She began rowing with two paddles, till she came
in on an island that was in the sea.   There was
a great giant on the shore.   " Have you got
anything for me to-night ? "

" I have not," said she ;   " but I'll have it
to-morrow night.   The son of the King of Erin
is with me to-night.   I shall have him for you
to-morrow night."

They went to the house.   " Here is the comb
I gave him to-night : it is yours."

The giant opened a chest.   He left the comb
in the bottom of the chest.   The red man was
standing by the chest.   When the giant left the
comb in it, the red man took it and put it in
his pocket.   The house was full of goats.   She
went to milk the goats, till she milked one part
of milk, and one part of blood.   She got the
supper ready.   That was the stuff they took.
The giant drew out an iron harrow and the
skin of a white mare.   They lay upon that till
morning.   When the day came she arose and
went away drawing to the sea.   The red man
followed her.   When she came to the boat she
put it in the water.   She went into it.   The

red man followed her on the sea. He was dashing water on her with the sword. She did not know what was delaying her. When they got home the red man went to his master. He asked him was he asleep. The king's son said he was not.

"I have saved your head to-night. Here is the comb. Put it in your pocket."

He put it in his pocket. The red man went to bed. When breakfast was ready in the morning the bell rang. They rose and they washed. When they were taking their breakfast she came down from the top of the house.

"Have you got the comb I gave you yesterday ? "

He put his finger in his pocket. He threw the comb to her. When she saw he had the comb to get she went by with one sweep. She broke the half of what was on the table. "I have a third of your daughter won," said the son of the King of Ireland.

" You have," said the king ; " you are the best champion ever came into my house."

They went hunting that day. When they came home they were making fun together till suppertime. When they were taking their supper, the beautiful woman came to them. She threw a pair of scissors to him : " Unless you have them for me to-morrow, I will have your head."

11

He took the scissors. He put them in his pocket. When they were going to bed said the red man to his master, " Look and see if you have the scissors."

" I have not," said his master.

" It's bad for you to lose them."

He went lamenting. The red man was comforting him till he got him to bed. When he slept, the red man went out. He put on the dark cloak and the slippery shoes, and took the sword of light. He stood outside the door. It was not long till she came out. She went down to the sea. She took a shell out of her pocket. She threw it on the sea and made a boat of it. She went to the island. The giant was on the shore.

" Have you got anything for me to-night ? "

" I have not," she said ; " but I shall have the son of the King of Erin to-morrow night." They went to the house. " Here are the scissors I gave him to-night. They are yours."

The giant opened a chest. He put the scissors in the bottom of the chest. The red man was standing by. When the giant put the scissors in the chest, the red man took them and put them in his pocket.

They took their supper. The giant pulled out the harrow and the skin of the white mare. They lay upon that till morning. In the morning she

went to the sea. The red man followed her.
She put her boat on the water. She went into it.
The red man followed her. He dashed in water
on her with the sword. When they got home,
the red man went to his master. He asked him
was he asleep? The king's son said he was not.

"I have saved your head this night. Here are
the scissors for you."

In the morning, when breakfast was ready, she
came down from the top of the house. She was
wet and dripping. She asked him had he the
scissors to give her. He put his hand in his
pocket. He threw her the scissors. She gave
one sweep. She did not leave a bit of delf on
the table she did not break in her rage. The
king's son said to the king he had two-thirds of
his daughter won.

"You have," said the king; "and I hope you
will win her altogether. I am tired of her."

They went hunting that day till night came.
When supper was ready, she came down with a
flight.

"Unless you have the last lips I shall kiss this
night, I'll have your head."

"It's hard for me," said the king's son, "to
know what are the last lips you kiss."

He was so troubled he did not know what to
do. The red man was comforting him till he got
him to bed. Then he went out. She came out.

She went to the island. When she got in on the island the giant was bellowing on the shore.

"Have you anything for me?" said the giant.

"I will never give you anything more. You let the comb go; you let the scissors go: he had the two to give me in the morning. To-night I put on him obligations for something he won't have to give me: that is, the last lips I shall kiss this night—and those are your lips."

She went to milk the goats. She mixed a part of blood, and a part of milk. She made ready the supper. They ate and drank enough. He got the iron harrow and the skin of the white mare. They lay upon that till morning. When the day came upon the morrow she kissed him three times.

"Those are the last lips I shall kiss. He won't have them to give me to-morrow."

She rose and she went. When she went out the red man whisked the head off the giant. He put a knot in the ear. He threw it over his shoulder. He was on the shore as soon as she was. She went into the boat. She was drawing to home. He went out after her. Much as he drenched her the nights before, twice as much did he drench her this night. They went home. The red man came to his master in bed,

"Are you asleep, master?"

"I am not now," said the king's son.

"Here are the last lips she kissed last night, and, by my faith, they were ugly lips for a lady to be kissing."

He took the head and threw it under the bed. When breakfast was ready in the morning she came down with a flight. She asked him,—

"Where are the last lips that I kissed last night?"

He put his hand under the bed. He took hold of the giant's head. He threw it over at her feet. When she saw the giant was dead she gave one sweep, and she left not a chair or a table, nor anything on the table, she did not make smash of, so great was her anger.

"I have your daughter all won now," said the king's son.

"You have; and you are the best champion that came under my roof ever."

"Well, we'll go hunting to-day," said the red man. They went hunting. The red man cut three bundles of rods. He made three flails. When they came home, "Now," said he, "bring your daughter out here."

The king brought her out. "Tie her hands and feet," said the red man, "and leave her lying there." The king left her lying. The red man gave one flail to the king, and one to his master.

"Strike you the first blow."

The king struck the first blow. The three were striking her for a long time. A blaze of fire came out of her mouth. "Strike ye more. There is more in her."

They struck till another lump of fire came out of her mouth. "Strike," said the red man, "there is one more in her."

They struck till the third came. "Now," said the red man, "strike her no more. Those were three devils that came out of her. Loose her now; she is as quiet as any woman in the world."

They loosed her and put her to bed. She was tired after the beating.

The priest of the pattens and the clerk of the bells came. The pair were married. The red man stayed with them a year and a day. A young son was born to them. When the day and the year were up the red man said it was time for him to be going.

"I don't know what I'll do after you," said the king's son.

"Oh, make no delay," said the red man; "the hire is just."

"It is just," said the king's son.

He made two halves of all he gained since he hired him. "I will give you my child all," said he; "I think it a pity to go to cut him in two."

"I will not take him all," said the red man; "I will not take but my bargain."

The king's son took a knife and was going to cut. "Stop your hand," said the red man. "Do you remember the day you were going past the churchyard? There were four men in the churchyard. They had a corpse, and they were arguing about the debts that were on the corpse. They were not willing to bury the corpse till the debts were paid. You had five pounds. You gave them to bury the corpse. It was I was in the coffin that day. When I saw you starting on your journey I went to you to save you, you were that good yourself. I bestow on you your child and your money. Health be with you and blessing. You will set eyes upon me no more."

GRIG.

Narrator, JACK GILLESPIE, *Glen, Glencolumkille,*
co. Donegal.

MORROCHA heard that Grig would live for ever, until he was killed without sin. He left home to put Grig to death; and he and his boy went one day on the hill, and there came on them rain and mist, and they went astray till night came; and the boy said to Morrocha, "We shall be out this night."

"Oh, we shall not be," said Morrocha. And he went and looked through the mist. "I think I see a turf stack: it is not possible we are near a house?" They went on for another bit, and Morrocha stood: "I think," said he, "I hear the lowing of a cow."

"We are near a house," said the boy, "and we'll get into the byre."

Morrocha stood up, and he felt the breath of a man, and he came to him. "Bless you," said Morrocha.

"My blessing to you," said the man; "for if you did not bless me, I would have your head or you would have mine."

"The death-bands on you," said Morrocha; "sorry I am I came to ask shelter of you."

Said Theegerje, "I have no shelter to give you. There is not a house nearer to you than the house of Grig, and that is seven miles away; and if you go there don't tell that you have seen me. I am his servant boy, and Grig is lying on the one bed for seven years, and if you go there tell him you are the best doctor ever stepped."

Morrocha went on then, and when he came to Grig's house, said Grig, "If it were not that you are a good doctor, I would cut the head from you."

"The death-bands on you," said Morrocha; "sorry I am I came to cure you, above and beyond the report I heard about you at home and abroad."

"And," said Grig, "if I had Njuclas Croanj and my wife she would not be on your side."

She was sleeping at Grig's back in the bed, and he told her to get up, and she did not stir, and Grig lifted his hand and struck her on the jawbone and put it out of joint, and she awoke and she said, "What made you do that to me?"

"Be silent, woman; don't you see the Irish doctor that's come to cure me, and to see me hale and whole and as good as ever I was?"

"Musha, it's a poor place he's come to. There isn't a wisp dry or wet that isn't under your side, and we haven't a stool better than the floor, or a chair better than a lump of clay, and we haven't as much fire as would cook the wing of a butterfly."

"Be silent, woman," said Grig, "and take my old great coat and fix it under me."

She did that; and Theegerje came, and a load of faggots with him, and he put down a good fire, and Morrocha got food to eat, and when he warmed himself at the fire he was weary-wet, and he was falling asleep.

"The death-bands on you," said Grig; "you're not like a doctor, for you've never asked what kind of sickness is on me."

"It is not that," said Morrocha; "but there are numbers of people, and their blood runs all together when they see strangers."

"I am of them," said Grig.

"I was not going to feel your pulse until you got quiet."

When he became quiet Morrocha arose and felt his pulse.

"And great is the pity," said he, "that a fine man like you should be lying in that place on one bed, and I will cure you. If you got potatoes and butter, and ate the full of your fist, you would not be long sick."

"That's true," said Grig, "and if Njuclas Croanj gave me that I wouldn't be lying here."

Morrocha asked if they had any food in the house, and Njuclas Croanj said they had,—that Theegerje was just after coming from the mill, and that he had three pecks of oatmeal. And Morrocha bade them give him a peck of meal, and she gave him that. And he asked if there was any butter in the house, and she said there was. "Bring me down a crock of fresh butter," said he. And she brought that to him, and Morrocha mixed the meal and the butter up together, and he asked for a spoon, and he thrust the spoon into the dish.

"Do you see that?" said he.

"I see," said Grig.

"You won't get it," said Morrocha, "till you tell me what was the horde of people from whom you came."

"I will tell you that," said Grig. "I am Grig, son of Stubborn, son of Very-evil, Shanrach, son of Canrain, son of the Soldier, who made people loathe him greatly."

"The death-bands on you," said Morrocha. "Weren't they ugly names they had?"

"The death-bands on you," said Grig. "Isn't it you that are ugly? They were prosperous, blessed."

"I give in that they were," said Morrocha.

"It was ignorance made me say that. But what sort was that one, the son of the Soldier?"

"This," said Grig, "was one of the fathers who came before me; and the snout of a pig was on his forehead; and he had two daughters, whose names were Maywa, the big, Molloy's daughter, and the other's Sahwa, the big, daughter of Cricheen, and they went to Cornelius (?) the tailor, and they gathered the clippings the tailors threw away, and they made up two lying books of them, and they failed to make the books agree upon one story; and they struck one another, and the father came, and they struck their father and cut him; and he went, and he in his blood, and the pig's snout on his forehead, and there is not one that saw him, but they would flee from him in thousands. And at last they got the two books to agree upon one story, and when the clergy heard they had the books, they desired to possess them, and they would not give them. And they banished them; and if they banished them we will not leave the night supperless."

"And now," said Morrocha, "I will give you supper." And he went and gave the dish to Grig, and he ate the peck of meal and the butter mixed together. "Now," said the other, "thirst will come on you; the butter was saltish, but do not drink a drop until I gather herbs that will help your sickness." He went and the boy, and Njuclas

Croanj and Theegerje with them, and they put down a big pot full of water before they went, and Morrocha gathered the full of a basket of hellebore (?) and he gathered tormentil, and he went into the house with Njuclas Croanj and Theegerje, and he bade them put the herbs into the pot and boil them, and when he grew thirsty to give him some of the liquor to drink, and, if he wished, some of the stalks to eat, "and I will gather more, and will come in to see if he is getting better."

And Grig took a great thirst, and he set to drinking what was in the pot, and he drank it all; and when Njuclas Croanj went in, Morrocha and his boy went away; and when Grig drank the last of what was in the pot, he burst as he lay on the bed; and when Njuclas Croanj saw he was dead, she followed Morrocha; but since the Lord was with Morrocha, he escaped.

THE LITTLE GIRL WHO GOT THE BETTER OF THE GENTLEMAN.

Narrator, P. M'GRALE, *Achill, co. Mayo.*

THERE was an old man with a little girl of seven years, and he was begging; and he came to a gentleman, and begged of him; and the gentleman said it would be better for him to go and earn wages than to be as he was—begging; and the man said he would go, and willingly, if he got any one to pay him, and the other said he would himself give him pay, and a house to live in for himself, and for the little girl to come to and wash and cook for him. He gave them the house, and they went to live in it.

They were not long there when the gentleman came to the little girl one day, and thought to take liberties with her, but she kept herself free from him. When he saw that, he went to his workmen, and he spoke to her father, and said to him that he would hang him at twelve o'clock next day unless he told him which there was the greater number of, rivers or banks. His intention was to put the old man to death, that he might have his way with the little girl. And the old man went home sorrowful and troubled, and his daughter asked him what ailed him, and he told her he was to be hung at twelve o'clock next day unless he could tell which there was the greater number of, rivers or banks.

"Oh, don't be sorrowful," said his daughter, "eat your supper, and sleep plenty, and eat your breakfast in the morning, and when you are going to work, I will tell you."

In the morning said she to him, "Say, when he asks you the question, that there is not a river but has two banks."

When he went to work the master came and asked him, "Which is there the greater number of, rivers or banks?"

"There is not a river," said he, "but has two banks."

"Your question is answered; but you must tell me to-morrow the number of the stars."

And he went home in the evening sorrowful and troubled. And his daughter asked him what ailed him, and he told her. She bade him not to be sorrowful, for she would tell him in the morning. And in the morning he went to his work, and his master came and asked him to count the number of the stars; and he said,—

" I will, if you put posts under them."

And he could not do that, but he said,—

" I will hang you at twelve to-morrow, if you don't give me the measure of the sea in quarts."

And he went home to his daughter and told her, and in the morning, as he was going to work, she said,—

" Let him stop the rivers that are going into the sea or out of it, and you will measure it in quarts."

So he gave that answer to his master, and his master could not stop the rivers.

Then he asked for the little girl in marriage, and the old man told him not to be making fun of the little girl, she was not fit for him.   He would get a lady.

" I will not do that," said he, " you must give her to me to marry."

" Well, I must see the little girl; she will know what she will do."

He went to his daughter and told her what the gentleman said, and the little girl answered her father, and said to him,—

" I will marry him, but he must give me a writing under his hand that on the day when he puts me away he must give me my choice of all that's in his house, to take away three loads with me."

And he said he would give her that, and she got it in his handwriting and signed by the lawyer.

Then the little girl came and lived in his house with him until she had two children.

At that time there was a dispute in the village between two men, one of whom had a horse, and the other a mare and a foal, and the three beasts used to be together. And the man who owned the horse said that the foal belonged to the horse; and the man of the mare, said no, that the foal was his; and the man who owned the horse put law on the man who owned the mare, and they left it to arbitration; and the man who was brought in to decide was the gentleman, who said he would settle it between them. And this is the judgment he gave, "He would put the three beasts into an empty house, and he would open two doors, and which ever of the two the foal followed, she should be with that one." And he (did so) and opened the doors, and struck each beast, and prodded the horse; and the horse went out first and the foal followed him. Then the foal was given to the man who owned the horse.

All was well till there came some gentlemen to the house. They went out hunting. And when they were a while gone the woman took a fishing-rod, and she went fishing in the lake, and she was catching white trout until she saw the company coming, and she turned her back to the lake, and she began casting her line on the dry land. When her husband saw that, he went towards her, away

12

from the other people, and he came and said it was a great wonder she should be casting her line on the dry ground and the lake on the other side of her; and she said it was a great wonder that a horse without milk should have a foal. That made him very angry, and he said on the spot,—

"After your dinner get ready and go from me."

'Will you give me what you promised?"

"I will give it."

After dinner, when the gentlemen were gone, he told her to be going, and she stood up and took with her her own child as a load and laid it down outside the door. She came in and took the second child as her load and put it outside. She came and she said, "I believe yourself are the load that's nearest to me." And she threw her arms round him and took him out as her third load. "You are now my own," said she, "and you cannot part from me."

"Oh! I am content," said he, "and I promise I will not part from you for ever."

They lived together then, and she took her father into the house, and he was with her until he died. They had a long life after.

GILLA OF THE ENCHANTMENTS.

Narrator, P. M'GRALE, *Dugort, Achill, co. Mayo.*

THERE was a king in Ireland and his wife, and they had but one daughter, whose name was Gilla of the Enchantments, and she had a magic coat that her mother left her when she died. And there was a man courting her whose name was George nǎ Riell, and the two were courting.

When her mother died the king made a fair and beautiful greenawn for his three sons on an island in the midst of the sea, and there he put them to live; and he sent his daughter to them with food every evening.

It was not long after that till he married another wife, and by this wife he had three daughters. She was one day walking in the garden, and she got the corner of her apron under her foot and she fell.

"May neither God nor Mary be with you," said the hen-wife.

" Why do you say that ? " said the queen.

" Because the wife that was here before was better than you."

" Was there a wife before me ? "

" There was ; and that one is her daughter, and there are three sons also in an island in the sea, and the daughter goes every night to them with food."

" What shall I do with the three of them, to put them to death ? "

" I'll tell you," said the hen-wife, " if you will do what I advise you."

" I will do it," said she.

" Promise a dowry to your eldest daughter if she will follow the (other) daughter out when she is going with food to her brothers."

And she sent her daughter after the one who was going with food ; but she looked behind her and saw the other coming, and she made a bog and a lake between them, so big that she went astray. She came to her mother, and told her she was wandering all the night, and the mother went to the hen-wife again and told her that her daughter had not made her way to the men ; and the hen-wife said to her, " Promise a dowry to your second daughter."

And she did this, and the second daughter followed as the first did, and fared in the same way, and she came and told her mother. And the mother went again to the hen-wife, and told her, and asked what she ought to do, and the hen-wife said, " Promise the dowry to your third daughter."

And the third daughter followed Gilla of the Enchantments when she was going with the food ; and she did not look behind her till she came to the house; and she put a pot of water down, and cut off the heads of her three brothers, and washed them, and put them on their shoulders again. And the half-sister was at the window looking on at everything she did, and she went home through the sea, before the sea returned together ; and when they ate their supper, her sister came home.

The mother went in the morning to the hen-wife and told her the third woman had succeeded, and had learned everything. And she asked her what she should do.

' Say, now, that your daughter is going to be married, and ask Gilla for the loan of the coat. She will not know that the power of the coat will be gone if she gives it away. So long as she keeps the coat herself she can do everything ; there are spells on the coat that the sea must open before it, without closing after it ; but she does not know that the spell of the coat will be lost."

She gave the loan of the coat to her half-sister, but instead of going to be married this is what she did. When night came she put the coat on and went to the house of her half-brothers, knocked at the door, and asked them to open it.   And one of the brothers said, "That is not my sister."   But another looked out of the window and saw the coat and recognised it, and he opened the door and let her in.   She cut the three heads off, and took them three quarters of a mile and put them into a hole in the ground, and went back to her mother and told her she had killed the three.   She gave the coat back to Gilla of the Enchantments, and Gilla went in the evening to her brothers with food, and whatever sort of fastening the other one put on the door she could not open it, but had to go in by the window, and she found her three brothers dead.

She wept and she screamed and pulled the hair from her head in her lamentations, till the whiteness of the day came upon the morrow.   She had not one head of the heads to get; but she followed the trace of the blood, and three quarters of a mile from the house were they in the place where they were buried.   She dug them up, and took them to her, and washed and cleaned them, as was her wont, and put them on the bodies, but down they fell.   She had to take them up at last, and cry to God to do something to them, that she might see them alive.   And there were made of them three water-dogs (? otters) and she made another of herself.   They were going in that way for a time, and then they made themselves into three doves, and she made of herself another dove. They were going forward and she was following, and the four came and settled on the gable of the house, and in the morning the man said to his wife,—

" There is a barrel of water. Let it be wine with you in the evening."

(He had a thought that it was not the right woman he had got.)

Then said one of the brothers to the sister,—

"Go in, and do good in return for evil, and make wine of the water."

She went down, and when she got in, and she in the shape of a dove, the old blind wise man, who was lying on the bed under the window, got his sight, and he saw her dipping her finger in the water and making of it wine cold and wholesome.

And in the morning the man said to his wife,—

"Here is a barrel of water. Let it be wine with you in the evening."

And the second brother said to his sister,—

"Go in, and do good in return for evil, and make wine of the water."

She went down, and when she went in at the window, and she in the shape of a dove, the old wise blind man, who was lying on the bed under the window, got his sight, and saw her dipping her finger in the water and making it wine cold and wholesome.

And in the morning on the third day the wise old man spoke to the king, and said to him that he had seen a beautiful woman come in by the window on two days, and that he got his sight when she came in and lost it when she went out ; and (said he) "Stretch yourself here to-day, and when she comes in and makes wine of the water, catch her as she is going out."

And he did so, and the third brother said to his sister,—

"Go down to-day, and do good in return for evil, and make the wine."

And she did this ; and as she was going out the man caught her. And when her brothers heard that she was caught they went away. And she asked him to give her leave to take just one look at her brothers.

"Here's the corner of my apron."

And he took hold of the corner of her apron, and she left him the apron and went away after her brothers. When they saw her coming again they waited for her, and she asked them if there was anything at all in the world that would make them alive again ; and they said there was one thing only and that hard it was to do.

"What is it ? " said she, " and I will try it."

" To make three shirts of the ivy-leaves in a day and a year, without uttering a word of speech or shedding a single tear, for if you weep* we shall lose one member of our members."

And she said to them to make a little hut for her in the wood, and they made the hut and went away and left her there. She was not long till she began to get material for the shirts, and she began to make them ; and she was not long in the house when George nă Riell came to her, and he was with her till she had a child to him.

A young man was in the wood one day and a dog with him, and the dog took him to the place where the woman was; and the man saw the woman and the child there, and he went home and told the queen that there was a beautiful woman in the wood. And she went and took the dog with her, as if the dog was with George nă Riell. She went in and found the woman and the babe, and she killed the babe and caught some of the blood, and mixed the blood and ashes up to-gether and made a cake, and she sought to put a piece of the bread into the woman's mouth. And the woman dropped one tear from her eye ; but the other went away home to her wedded husband, and she said to him that great was the shame for him to have children by that woman, and that she had had to kill her own child and eat it.

* The narrator knew his story imperfectly as regards this point, for she did shed one tear; but whether the brothers lost an eye in consequence he was not sure.

"It is not possible," said he, "that she has killed my babe."

"She killed and she ate."

He went to her and found the child dead; but she did not speak a word to him. He said then he would burn her at twelve o'clock on the next day, and that he would put a tree of one foot and hang her on it. He commanded that every one should come in the morning with sods of turf and sheets of paper and everything to make a fire. And he put the tree standing, and she was brought and put up on the top of the tree; and she was sewing during this time. When it was twelve o'clock, sign was given she should be hung, and an old man in the crowd asked them to give her another hour by the clock; and when the hour was passed he asked again that they should give her a half-hour; the woman in it (he said) was under gassa. "You see that it is not her life that is troubling her, but that she is always sewing."

It was not long till they saw a black cloud coming through the air, and they saw three things in the cloud coming.

"Well," said the old man, "there are three angels from heaven, or three devils from hell, coming for her soul."

There were three black ravens coming, and their mouths open, and as it were fire out of their mouths, till the three black ravens came and lay

in their sister's bosom, and she on the top of
the tree, and she put the three shirts on them,
and said,—

"Finn, Inn, and Brown Glegil, show that I am
your sister, for in pain am I to-day."

They took hold of her and lifted her down from
the tree, and the brothers told George nǎ Riell
everything that the half-sister had done, first that
she killed the three of them, and afterwards that
it was she that killed their sister's child.

Then she was put up on the tree, and she was
hung, and then thrown into the fire. And they
went home, and George nǎ Riell married Gilla of
the Enchantments and took her into his own
house, and they spent the rest of their life as
is right.

I don't know what happened to them since
then.

THE WOMAN WHO WENT TO HELL.

Narrator, P. MINAHAN, *Malinmore, Glencolumkille, co. Donegal.*

THERE was a woman coming out of her garden with an apron-full of cabbage. A man met her. He asked her what she would take for her burden. She said it was not worth a great deal, that she would give it to him for nothing. He said he would not take it, but would buy it. She said she would only take sixpence. He gave her the sixpence. She threw the cabbage towards him. He said that was not what he bought, but the burden she was carrying. Who was there but the devil? She was troubled then. She went home and she was weeping. It was a short time until her young son was born. He was growing till he was eighteen years old. He was out one day and fell, and never rose up till he died. When they were going to bury him, they took him to the people's house (*i.e.*, the chapel). They left him there till morning.

There was a man among the neighbours who had three daughters. He took out a box of snuff to give (the men) a pinch. The last man to whom the box went round left the box on the altar. They went home. When the man was going to bed he went looking for his box. The box was not to be got. He said he had left it behind him in the people's house. He said he would not sleep that night until he got a pinch. He asked one of his daughters to go to the people's house and bring him the box that was on the altar. She said there was loneliness on her. He cried to the second woman, would she go? She said she would not go; that she was lonely. He cried to the third, would she go? And she said she would go; that there was no loneliness on her in his presence (*i.e.*, of the corpse).

She went to the people's house. She found the box. She put it in her pocket. When she was coming away she saw a ring at the end of the coffin. She caught hold of it till it came to her. The end came from the coffin. The man that was dead came out. He enjoined on her not to be afraid.

"Do you see that fire over yonder? If you are able, carry me to that fire."

"I am not able," said she.

"Be dragging me with you as well as you can."

She put him on her back. She dragged him till they came to the fire.

"Draw out the fire," said he, "and put me lying in the midst of it; fix up the fire over me. Anything of me that is not burnt put the fire on it again."

He was burning till he was all burnt. When the day was coming she was troubled on account of what she had seen during the night. When the day grew clear there came a young man, who began making fun with her.

"I have not much mind for fun on account of what I have seen during the night."

"Well, it was I who was there," said the young man.

"I would go to heaven if I could get an angel made by you left in my father's room."

Three quarters (of a year) from that night she dressed herself up as if she was a poor woman. She went to his father's house and asked for lodging till morning. The woman of the house said that they were not giving lodging to any poor person at all. She said she would not ask but a seat by the fire. The man of the house told her to stay till morning. She stopped. They went both to lie down. She sat by the fire. In the course of the night she went into the room, and there she had a young son. He, *i.e.*, her husband, came in at the window in the shape of a white dove. He dressed the child. The child began to cry. The woman of the house heard the crying. She would wager the lady had left a baby after her. She rose to get out of the bed. Her husband told her to lie quiet and have patience. She got up in spite of him. The door of the room was shut. She looked in through the keyhole. He was standing on the floor. She perceived it was her son who was there. She cried to him, was it he that was there? He said it was.

"One glance of your eye has sent me for seven years to hell."

"I will go myself in your place," said his mother.

She went then to go to hell. When she came to the gate, there came out steam so that she was burnt and scalded. It was necessary for her to return. "Well," said the father, "I will go in your place." It was necessary for him to return. The young man began to weep. He said he must go himself. The mother of the child said that she would go.

"Here is a ring for you," said he. "When thirst comes on you, or hunger, put the ring in your mouth; you will feel neither thirst nor hunger. This is the work that will be on you— to keep down the souls; they are stewing and burning in the boiler. Do not eat a bit of food

there. There is a barrel in the corner, and all the
food that you get throw into the barrel."

She went to hell then. She was keeping down
the souls in the boiler. They were rising in leaps
out of it. All the food she got she threw into the
barrel till the seven years were over. She was
making ready to be going then. The devil came
to her. He said she could not go yet awhile till
she had paid for the food she had eaten. She
said she had not eaten one morsel of his share :
" All that I got, it is in the barrel." The devil
went to the barrel. All he had given her was
there for him.

" How much will you take to stay seven years
more ? "

"Oh, I am long enough with you," said she ;
" if you give me the all that I can carry, I can
stay with you."

He said he would give it. She stopped. She
was keeping down the souls during seven years.
She was shortening the time as well as she could
till the seven years were ended. Then she was
going. When the souls saw she was going they
rose up with one cry, lest one of them should
be left. They went clinging to her ; they
were hanging to her hair all that were in the
boiler. She moved on with her burden. She
had not gone far when a lady in a carriage
met her.

" Oh ! great is your burden," said the lady ;
" will you give it to me ? "

" Who are you ? " said she.

" I am the Virgin Mary."

" I will not give it to you."

She moved on with herself. She had not gone
far when a gentleman met her.

" Great is your burden, my poor woman ; will
you give it to me ? "

" Who are you ? " said she.

" I am God," said he.

" I will not give my burden to you."

She went on with herself another while.
Another gentlemen met her.

" Great is the burden you have," said the
gentleman ; " will you give it to me ? "

" Who are you ? " said she.

" I am the King of Sunday," said he.

" I will give my burden to you," said she. "No
rest had I ever in hell except on Sunday."

" Well, it is a good woman you are ; the first
lady you met it was the devil was there ; the
second person you met it was the devil was
there, trying if they could get your burden from
you back. Now," said God, " the man for whom
you have done all this is going to be married
to-morrow. He thought you were lost since you
were in that place so long. You will not know
till you are at home."

She did not know till she was at home. The house was full of drinking and music. She went to the fire. Her own son came up to her.

She was making him wonder she was so worn and wasted. She told the child to go to his father and get a glass of whisky for her to drink. The child went crying to look for his father. He asked his father to give him a glass of whisky. His father gave it. He came down where she was by the fire. He gave her the glass. She drank it, there was so much thirst on her. The ring that her husband gave her she put in the glass.

"Put your hand over the mouth of the glass; give it to no one at all till you hand it to your father."

The lad went to his father. He gave him the glass. The father looked into it, and saw the ring. He recognised the ring.

"Who has given you this?" said he.

"A poor woman by the fire," said the lad.

The father raised the child on his shoulders that he might point out to him the woman who had given him the ring. The child came to the poor woman.

"That is the woman," said he, "who gave me the ring."

The man recognised her then. He said that hardly did he know her when she came so worn and wasted. He said to all the people that he would never marry any woman but this one ; that she had done everything for him ; that his mother sold him to the devil, and the woman had earned him back ; that she had spent fourteen years in hell, and now she had returned.

This is a true story. They are all lies but this one.

THE KING WHO HAD TWELVE SONS.

Narrator, JOHN MCGINTY, *Valley, Achill Island.*

HE went down to the river every day and killed a salmon for each one of them. He saw a duck on the river and twelve (young) birds with her; and she was beating the twelfth away from her. He went to the old druid and asked what was the cause why the duck was beating away the twelfth bird from her.

"It was this," said the old druid; "she gave the bird to God and the Djachwi."

"Well, I have twelve sons," said the king; "I will give one of them to God and to the Djachwi, as the duck is giving one of her birds to God and the Djachwi. The twelve are going to school, and you must tell me which of them it is best for me to give away."

"Whichever of them is last at the gate in the evening, that is the man you will give away; and whatever money you have left out to give him throw it to him over the gate, and tell him he must go and seek his own fortune."

The younger children were running on first to the house, being hungry, and the eldest was coming, reading a book, after them. The father was standing at the gate on the inside, and he threw him a purse of money, and told him he must go seek his fortune, that he gave him to God and to the Djachwi.

He went and spent that night with the old druid. He rose in the morning and washed his face, and prayed to God to put him in luck again until evening. He gave a good heap of the gold to the old druid. The old druid gave him a card and a bridle, and told him that any beast he would rub the card to, if his skin was full of disease, would be cured.* He went away that morning and he met with a king upon the road. The king asked him,—

" What are you seeking ? "

" I am seeking a master," said he.

" Your like is what I am wanting," said the king. " I have three hundred horses and there is not one of them fit to put to my carriage, they are so full of lumps in their skin."

" I am able to cure them," said the other.

" How much do you ask till the end of a day and a year ? "

" I'll be asking of you nothing at all but the

* It must be supposed that the druid gave him further directions for his conduct as appears by the sequel.

beast that comes and puts the head in this bridle mine."

" Very well," said the king.

He was a good serving-boy, and he minded the horses. He was not two days with his master when two of them were cured, fit to go with the carriage. He went every evening to an old couple, and he used to get news in plenty from them.

" Did you hear the great news there is to-night ? "

" I did not hear. What is the news ? "

" The daughter of the King of the great Wren is to be devoured to-morrow by a piast." *

" I did not hear it," said he.

"Was it in a wood or a hole in the ground you've been that you didn't hear it ? Gentle and simple of the three islands are to be there to-morrow to look at the piast swallowing her—at twelve o'clock to-morrow."

(The next day) when he found that every one was gone to the place where the piast was to come on land, he called out for his second best suit of clothes, and it came to him with a leap ; and he shook the bridle, and the ugliest pony in the stables came to him and put her head into the bridle. "Be up riding on me with a jump" (said the pony)

* Piast is a Gaelic monster, not exactly equivalent to either serpent or dragon.

lowering himself on his two knees. He gave his face to the way and he would overtake the wind of March that was before him, and the wind of March that was after would not overtake him. When he came in sight of the place where the gathering was, the piast was coming till she was half upon the land ; and he and the piast went fighting, till he tore her with his mouth and feet.

He came back and gave his face to the way, and he ran so near to the place where the king's daughter was to be swallowed that she caught the boot from the foot of the man who was riding on the pony. He came home and attended to his horses, and no one knew who was the man who was mounted on the pony that killed the piast. She proclaimed a gathering of all the men in the three islands, that she might see who the man was whom the shoe fitted. There was not a man at all coming whom the shoe would fit, and she was not going to marry any man but the one whom the shoe fitted. The old man said it was right for him to go to her to see if the shoe would fit him. He called for the suit of clothes that he wore on the day when the pony killed the piast, and he went to her (the king's daughter). She knew him at once. The shoe was in her hand, and it leaped from her hand till it went on his foot.

" You are the man that was on the pony on the

day that he killed the piast, and you are the man whom I will marry."

He was seven nights and seven days at feast and festival, and they were married on the eighth day. They spent that night part in talking and part in story-telling ; till the early day came and the clear brightness on the morrow morning.

He said to her that he would be riding in the morning on the pony ; and he was going, and he came on an apple of gold upon the strand, and the pony told him not to take up the apple or it would give him abundance of trouble.

" Whatever trouble it may give me I will take it up ! "

He went home and the pearl of gold with him. In the morning he went to the old druid, and the old druid told him that it was the daughter of a king of the eastern world, who lost it from her hair ;—that there was a pearl of gold on every rib of hair upon her head, and that she and her twelve attendant women were bathing in such a place the day she lost it.

" I will never stop," said he, "till I see the woman who lost it."

The pony told him she was hard to see.

" There are seven miles of hill on fire to cross before you come to where she is, and there are seven miles of steel thistles, and seven miles of sea for you to go over. I told you to have nothing

to do with the apple. All the same it is as good
for you to go riding on me till we try to go to
her place."

He went on his two knees, and he went riding
on him, till he crossed the seven miles of hill on
fire, and the seven miles of steel thistles, and the
seven miles of sea. When they came to the castle
in which she was, there was a great dinner that
day with her, and a great gathering of company.
There were three-and-twenty feet of moat to cross
before the pony could get in. He rose with a
high leap and crossed the three-and-twenty feet.
He came down on the inside of the moat, and a
report went in (to the castle) that such and such a
stranger was there ; and she heard it and sent one
of her servants to him. He told the servant he
could not go in till he got leave to put the pony
in the stable. She herself came out to him, with
a golden goblet in her hand full of wine, and she
offered it to him ; but he said he would be obliged
to her if she would drink of it first. She drank
some of the wine first, and then held it out to
him ; and what he did was to leap again upon the
pony, and throw his arm round her waist, and lift
her up beside him on the pommel ; and the pony
gave his head towards the gates and crossed out
beyond them, and made no stop till he came to
their own castle with the lady.

"Now," said the pony, "strike a blow with

your rod of druidism upon me, and make of me a rock of stone, and whatever time at all you are in need of me, you have nothing to do but strike another blow on me, and I am up as I was before."

The woman was with him then; and the young queen he first married did not know there was such a person in the castle till the hen-wife told her. "Well!" said the hen-wife, "do you know what to do? He has no regard for you beside the other. There is an apple of gold on every rib of hair upon her head. You and he will be (playing cards) together to-night, and you will win the first game, and you will put him under bonds to go and bring you the black horse of the bank.

The two went playing that night. She won the first game, and he was to bring her the black horse of the bank. He went to the pony and struck a blow with his rod of druidism on him, and told her the news, that she put him under bonds to bring her the black horse of the bank. "I told you the first day," said the pony, "to leave the pearl alone, or it would give you abundance of trouble; you must go now and cover me with leather all over, and put pitch and tar on the outside of the leather. I will then go down to the cliff to fight with the black horse of the bank, till I see if I'll be able to bring him to you.

There is not a bit that he takes out of me that he will not get the full of his mouth of leather and pitch and tar, to my ribs."

He went down, and he and the horse were fighting till he brought him down from the cliff to him, and he brought him home to his wife. She went then again to the hen-wife, to get more information from her. The hen-wife told her that unless she could win another game on him, and put him under bonds to bring her the skin of the wild pig from the eastern world, he and this young queen would put her to death. The two went playing that night, and he won the first game from her, and she said to him, " Give your judgment now." "I percêive," said he, " that if it was you who had to give the first judgment, you would give a brief judgment on me. But now I put you under bonds to go, and not to sleep a wink, but for one night only in the one house, till you bring me the heads of the three black ravens that are in the eastern world."

She arose in the morning and went to the hen-wife, and told her : and the hen-wife said, " She had plenty of trouble before her ere she got the three black ravens from the eastern world. But now I have three brothers who are three giants, and to-night you will be with the first of them. I will give you a ring that will take you on your way swiftly to the king, and when you

come to him you will give him the ring, and he
will know who gave it to you. And great will be
the welcome he will have for you, and he will
give you every knowledge as far as the next
brother."

She gave her the ring, and she was with him
that night, and he told her that "he himself was
as much as third of the world, that his second
brother was two-thirds of the world, and the third
brother three-thirds, and that all the birds of the
air were under high tribute to him."

She arose in the morning and washed her face
and hands, and prayed to God, to put her in
luck; and that night she was with the second
brother ; and the third night she was with the
third brother. She gave him the ring and he
recognised it, and said he had not seen his sister
for a hundred years. She told him the journey
she was going.* "To-morrow," said he, "they
are coming with their high tribute, and unless I
can get tidings from them I cannot give you
tidings." Then in the morning came all the
birds of the air and paid to him their tribute, all
except the eagle : "And great is my wonder,"
said he, "that the eagle is last to-day, and no
tidings are there with any other bird, unless it is
with the eagle." He blew a whistle, and it was
not long till he saw a black lump coming in the

* *i.e.,* the cause of her journey.

sky, and who was it but the eagle ! He told the
eagle he would remit to him the tribute of the
seven years, if he could give him tidings of the
three black ravens that are in the eastern world.
"Well !" said he, "it is a year and a day since I
saw them, and I'll take another year and a day
before I can come to you with account of them."
"You must wait here" (said he to the woman)
to the end of a year and a day till the eagle
comes back to me with news, and you will have
nothing to do but sit down."

When the day and the year were ended, the
eagle came back and the three black ravens with
him, and he gave them to the giant, and the
giant took them from him. "And now" (said
he) "when you go home he will ask you if you
have them, and you will say you have not ; and
he will say he believes you never went at all to
look for them, and you will take them with you
then, and show them to him and let them out of
your hand, and they will not stop till they come
to me here."

When she came home her husband said to her,—
"Have you the three ravens ? "

"If I promised to bring them to you, I did not
promise to give them to you." And she let them
away.

He went that night to the old druid he had
himself, and he told him the thing she said to

him. And the old druid told him that unless he
could succeed in banishing the hen-wife from the
castle she would bring utter destruction on himself
and the queen. " Go now, and there is not any
way to banish her but the way I tell you. Send
her word this night, and invite her to play cards
with you; and when you win the first game tell
her she must go to the Gruagach of the Apple
and bring to you the sword of light that is with
the King of Rye, and then she has not a single
chance of returning. The queen will have no
one to tell her anything without the hen-wife, and
you yourself and the other queen will be quiet
and untroubled together then."

He sent her word that night and she came, and
he asked her would she play a game of cards?
She said she would play : that great was the
practice she learned in the house of her father and
mother when she was young, and that she was
very proud that he paid her a compliment so great
as to invite her. He drew out a table and a pack
of cards, and the two sat down beside the table,
and it was five hundreds they had in the game.
He succeeded until she put out the five hundreds.

" Now," said the hen-wife, " give your judgment on me."

" I put you under bonds and under curse of a
year to go to the eastern world and to bring the
sword of light belonging to the King of Rye from

the eastern world, and not to sleep a wink, but one night only, in the one house before you come back again."

She went with herself, and stopped not till she came to the castle of the King of Rye in the eastern world, and knocked at the Cuillë Coric, and the King of Rye came out and asked her what she was seeking.

" I am seeking," said she, " your sword of light and the divided stone of your druidism."

" Well, do you not see on the hill yonder all the heads of the champions who came to seek them from me, and never went man of them back to tell the story? and you are come, a woman, to seek ! "

" Well," said she, " it was not under protection of your shield I came at all, but under the protection of my own shield and blade."

She and the King of Rye then went at one another, and the King of Rye was getting the better of her, and she asked him to give her quarter for her life till morning.

" Hold out your hand till I cut off the tips of your little finger that I may be able to recognise you, and you will not get quarter for your life but this turn, (not) if you come to-morrow."

She went with herself and stopped that night at the smith's house; and the smith said to her,—

" It's a bad journey you've come on your

two feet. Many's the good champion I've seen crossing yonder bridge, and a man of them to tell the story came back never. Unless you do the thing I tell you, you will get the like death. Go to-night," said he, " and rise in the morning, and I will give you a sword if you pay me for my service; and I will cut off the tip of the little finger on your other hand, and you will go to the hall-door at the time when he is at his breakfast, and he will ask you, ' Haven't you a sudden desire to die that you come to me so early ? ' "

She went in the morning to the hall-door of the King of Rye, and he said to her,—

" Sudden is your desire to die since you come to me so early, and haven't given me leave to eat my breakfast; but that is the thing that will make your own life shorter. Stretch out your hand that I may see if it was you were here yesterday."

She stretched out her two hands and he found the tips of her two little fingers were cut off, and he said she must have got advice from the smith when she did that. She took up from the ground the sword the smith gave her. When he saw the sword he begged for quarter for his life, for he knew the sword was equal to half the world, and that it was no good for him to fight against it. He said he would give her all he ever saw upon the earth, but would not face that sword she had.

" I am asking nothing of you except your sword of light and the divided stone of your druidism."

" Those are the two things that it is worst for me to part from."

He went in and brought them out to her, and she went with herself to the smith, and she spent that night at the smith's house, and gave him a good hansel of gold for the sword he gave her. " Now," said the smith, " though he put you under bonds to bring the sword to him, you did not promise more than to bring it to him. When you come to him and the things with you, and you take them up in your two hands and show them to him, you will say, though you promised to bring them to him, you did not promise to bring them for him and you will let them go, and they will be with me here in the winking of your eye. Unless they come back to me, the King of Rye will' put me to death, as he knows I gave you my sword ; and there will be peace made between him and me, and the quarrel between us will be at an end."*

*   *   *   *   *

And when the first wife saw the second wife

* The narrator's memory failed him at this point, and he was unable to relate the further developments of this remarkable game of plot and counterplot. Although the hen-wife was successful in the last event mentioned, it

with her own eyes, she could esteem herself no longer, and she died of a broken heart.

must be inferred that she was ultimately defeated. I believe there are other deficiencies in the story. One hears nothing more of the skin of the wild pig after its first mention, p. 203. The same remark applies to the Gruagach of the Apple, p. 206. On the other hand, "the divided stone of druidism" is brought in without explanation. It had not been asked for.

THE RED PONY.

Narrator, P. MINAHAN, *Malinmore, co. Donegal.*

THERE was a poor man there. He had a
great family of sons. He had no means
to put them forward. He had them at school.
One day, when they were coming from school, he
thought that whichever of them was last at the
door he would keep him out. It was the youngest
of the family was last at the door. The father
shut the door. He would not let him in. The
boy went weeping. He would not let him in till
night came. The father said he would never let
him in ; that he had boys enough.

The lad went away. He was walking till night.
He came to a house on the rugged side of a
hill on a height, one feather giving it shelter
and support. He went in. He got a place till
morning. When he made his breakfast in the
morning, he was going. The man of the house
made him a present of a red pony, a saddle, and
bridle. He went riding on the pony. He went
away with himself.

"Now," said the pony, "whatever thing you may see before you, don't touch it."

They went on with themselves. He saw a light before him on the high-road. When he came as far as the light, there was an open box on the road, and a light coming up out of it. He took up the box. There was a lock of hair in it.

"Are you going to take up the box?" said the pony.

"I am. I cannot go past it."

"It's better for you to leave it," said the pony.

He took up the box. He put it in his pocket. He was going with himself. A gentleman met him.

"Pretty is your little beast. Where are you going?"

"I am looking for service."

"I am in want of one like you, among the stable boys."

He hired the lad. The lad said he must get room for the little beast in the stable. The gentleman said he would get it. They went home then. He had eleven boys. When they were going out into the stable at ten o'clock each of them took a light but he. He took no candle at all with him.

Each of them went to his own stable. When he went into his stable he opened the box. He left it in a hole in the wall. The light was great.

It was twice as much as in the other stables. There was wonder on the boys what was the reason of the light being so great, and he without a candle with him at all. They told the master they did not know what was the cause of the light with the last boy. They had given him no candle, and he had twice as much light as they had.

" Watch to-morrow night what kind of light he has," said the master.

They watched the night of the morrow. They saw the box in the hole that was in the wall, and the light coming out of the box. They told the master. When the boys came to the house, the king asked him what was the reason why he did not take a candle to the stable, as well as the other boys. The lad said he had a candle. The king said he had not. He asked him how he got the box from which the light came. He said he had no box. The king said he had, and that he must give it to him ; that he would not keep him unless he gave him the box. The boy gave it to him. The king opened it. He drew out the lock of hair, in which was the light.

" You must go," said the king, " and bring me the woman, to whom the hair belongs."

The lad was troubled. He went out. He told the red pony.

" I told you not to take up the box. You will get more than that on account of the box.

When you have made your breakfast to-morrow, put the saddle and bridle on me."

When he made his breakfast on the morning of the morrow, he put saddle and bridle on the pony. He went till they came to three miles of sea.

"Keep a good hold now. I am going to give a jump over the sea. When I arrive yonder there is a fair on the strand. Every one will be coming up to you to ask for a ride, because I am such a pretty little beast. Give no one a ride. You will see a beautiful woman drawing near you, her in whose hair was the wonderful light. She will come up to you. She will ask you to let her ride for a while. Say you will and welcome. When she comes riding, I will be off."

When she came to the sea, she cleared the three miles at a jump. She came upon the land opposite, and every one was asking for a ride upon the beast, she was that pretty. He was giving a ride to no one. He saw that woman in the midst of the people. She was drawing near. She asked him would he give her a little riding. He said he would give it, and a hundred welcomes. She went riding. She went quietly till she got out of the crowd. When the pony came to the sea she made the three-mile jump again, the beautiful woman along with her. She took her home to the king. There was great joy on the king to see her. He took her into the parlour. She said to him, she would not marry any one until he would get the bottle of healing water that was in the eastern world. The king said to the lad he must go and bring the bottle of healing water that was in the eastern world to the lady. The lad was troubled. He went to the pony. He told the pony he must go to the eastern world for the bottle of healing water that was in it, and bring it to the lady.

"My advice was good," said the pony, "on the day you took the box up. Put saddle and bridle on me."

He went riding on her. They were going till they came to the sea. She stood then.

"You must kill me," said the pony ; "that, or I must kill you."

"It is hard to me to kill you," said the boy. "If I kill you there will be no way to myself."

He cut her belly down. He opened it up. She was not long opened when there came two black ravens and one small one. The two ravens went into the body. They drank their fill of the blood. When they came out the little raven went in. He closed the belly of the pony. He would not let the little bird come out till he got the bottle of healing water was in the eastern world. The ravens were very troubled. They were begging him to let the little bird out. He said he would not let it out till they brought him the bottle. They went to seek the bottle. They came back and there was no bottle with them. They were entreating him to let the bird out to them. He would not let the bird out till he got the bottle. They went away again for the bottle. They came at evening. They were tossed and scorched, and they had the bottle. They came to the place where the pony was. They gave the bottle to the boy. He rubbed the healing water to every place where they were burned. Then he let out the little bird. There was great joy on them to see him. He rubbed some of the healing water to the place where he cut the pony. He spilt a drop into her ear. She arose as well as she ever was. He had a little bottle in his pocket. He put some of the healing water into it. They went home.

When the king perceived the pony coming he rose out. He took hold of her with his two hands. He took her in. He smothered her with kisses and drowned her with tears : he dried her with finest cloths of silk and satin.

This is what the lady was doing while they were away. She boiled pitch and filled a barrel, and that boiling. Now she went beside it and stripped herself. She rubbed the healing water to herself. She came out ; she went to the barrel, naked. She gave a jump in and out of the barrel. Three times she went in and out. She said she would never marry any one who could not do the same. The young king came. He stripped himself. He went to the barrel. He fell half in, half out.

He was all boiled and burned. Another gentleman came. He stripped himself. He gave a jump into the barrel. He was burned. He came not out till he died. After that there was no one going in or out. The barrel was there, and no one at all was going near it. The lad went up to it and stripped himself. He rubbed the healing water on himself. He came to the barrel. He jumped in and out three times. He was watching her. She came out. She said she would never marry any one but him.

Came the priest of the pattens, and the clerk of the bells. The pair were married. The wedding lasted three nights and three days. When it was over, the lad went to look at the place where the pony was. He never remembered to go and see the pony during the wedding. He found nothing but a heap of bones. There were two champions and two young girls playing cards. The lad went crying when he saw the bones of the pony. One of the girls asked what was the matter with him. He said it was all one to her; that she cared nothing for his troubles.

"I would like to get knowledge of the cause why you are crying."

"It is my pony who was here. I never remembered to see her during the wedding. I have nothing now but her bones. I don't know what I shall do after her. It was she who did all that I accomplished."

The girl went laughing. "Would you know your pony if you saw her?"

"I would know," said he.

She laid aside the cards. She stood up.

"Isn't that your pony?" said she.

"It is," he said.

"I was the pony," said the girl, "and the two ravens who went in to drink my blood my two brothers. When the ravens came out, a little bird went in. You closed the pony. You would not let the little bird out till they brought the bottle of healing water that was in the eastern world. They brought the bottle to you. The little bird was my sister. It was my brothers were the ravens. We were all under enchantments. It is my sister who is married to you. The enchantments are gone from us since she was married."

THE NINE-LEGGED STEED.

Narrator, P. MINAHAN, *Malinmore, co. Donegal.*

THERE was a king and a queen. They had
but one son. The queen died. He married
another queen. The queen was good to the child.
She took care of him till he was a young man.
She sent him away to learn chivalry. When he
came home there was grèat joy on the queen.
When he had rested at home, he and the huntsman went hunting on the mountain. They found
no game at all. They came to the lake. They
sat down on a height beside the lake. They
saw three swans coming towards the height.
They rested on the lake. They swam in under
the place where they were sitting. They came on
the shore. They threw off them the transforming
caps. They arose the three maidens. One woman
of them was very comely. They came up to the
young men. The comely woman was there. She
and the king's son were talking until night.
When they were going she asked him would he

be there the next day. He said he would. The
women went on the shore. They put on the
transforming caps. They went away the three
swans. The young men came home. There
was great joy on the young queen. She asked
the huntsman what kind of sport they had. He
said they had none at all ; that three swans came
from the eastern direction ; that they had settled
on the lake ; that they swam in to the place where
they were sitting ; that they rose up on the
beach ; that they threw off the transforming caps ;
that they rose the three maidens ; that one of
them was very beautiful ; that he himself and the
king's son were talking with the girl.

The young queen said they were done with
his master. " I will give you five pounds if you
put the slumber-pin in his clothes. He will fall
asleep then. She won't get a word of talk from
him. He will be sleeping."

The young man said he would do it. They
took their supper. They went to lie down.
When day came they arose. They washed themselves. They took their breakfast. They went
hunting. They found no sport at all till they
came to the lake. They sat down on a pretty
hillock. They saw the three swans coming.
They settled on the lake. They came in on the
shore. They threw off them the transforming
caps. They rose the three maidens. When the

son of the king and the huntsman sat down, the huntsman put the slumber-pin in his clothes. He fell asleep. The girls came up. They sat by his side.

"Great is the sleep that's on your master to-day."

"That is no wonder for him," said the huntsman. "He does not sleep one night at home, but is out rambling and courting."

She was shaking him to wake him. She failed to wake him till it was time for her to be going. She said to the young man, "Tell your master we will come here to-morrow ; unless he is awake to-morrow to speak to us, we will come no more."

They went away then. They put on them the transforming caps. They went away again the three swans. The young man took out the slumber-pin from his master's clothes. He awoke then. They went home then. He was not speaking a word. The young queen asked the huntsman how it happened with him to-day? He said it happened well ; that he put him asleep to-day.

"A good man you are," said she. "Here are five pounds more for you. Do the same to morrow."

They took their supper. They went to lie down. When the day came on the morrow, they arose and took their breakfast. The king's son said to the huntsman that he would not go with him to-day ; that it was he was doing something or other to him.

" It is not I," said the huntsman.

The king's son went out. The huntsman followed him. When they were coming near the lake, he could not fasten the slumber-pin in him. When they were coming to the place where they sat he threw the slumber-pin. He got it fastened in his frock. He fell asleep on the instant. He took hold of him; he drew him to the place where they used to sit. He sat down by his side. The three swans came. They settled on the lake. They swam in to the shore. They threw off them the transforming caps. They rose the three maidens. They came again to the place where the young men were.

" Is your master asleep to-day ? "

" He is ; he has not slept a wink at home for three nights."

She was shaking him to try if she could wake him. She failed. When she was going, " Say to your master that he will never see sight of me while streams run or grass grows."

They went away then. The huntsman took the slumber-pin out. Then he awoke. He looked up at the sun. Night was at hand. He asked were the maidens there that day. The young man said they were.

" What did they say when they were going ? "

" They said you would never have a sight of them while streams run or grass grows."

" Don't come near me or I will kill you."

Fear would not let the huntsman come near him. They went home then. The young queen asked the young man were the maidens with them that day. The young man said they were.

" What did they say to you ? "

" They said you would not see a sight of them while streams run or grass grows."

" You are done with her," said the queen.

They took their supper then and went to lie down. When the day came he arose and washed. He took his breakfast. He said good-bye to them. He said he would not sleep a second time for one night in one house ; that he would wear his legs to his knees till he got one sight of that woman.

He went with himself then. He was walking till it was night. He saw not a house at all that would give him lodging. He saw one house on the side of a hill, one feather giving it support and shelter. He went into the house. A horse-beast. spoke to him from the side. He gave welcome to the son of the King of Erin.

" Go down to the fire and warm yourself; when you have warmed yourself, go to the room, and there is food and drink on the table : don't be afraid of anything at all. Nothing will happen to you till morning. When you have eaten enough come down and lie here on the grass under my head that I may talk with you."

He came down and sat on the grass : " Have no wonder at anything you see."

It was not long till he heard a troop coming into the house. Three seals came in. They came into the room. They threw off the transforming caps. They sat down to dinner. The son of the king wondered when he saw the three seals coming in. It was not long till he heard them talking and laughing. Said the eldest of them,—

" If I had the son of the King of Erin here I would give on him a gift. I would give him an apple. There is not a going astray, nor any (trouble), let him throw the apple in the air, there would come a court and castle in the track ; there would come food and drink in the track."

Said the second son, " If I had the son of the King of Erin here, I would give him a ring ; and there is not a battle or breaking that would come on him, let him raise the ring between himself and his (enemies) he would blind them and kill them all."

Said the son that was youngest, " If I had the son of the King of Erin here, I would give him the nine-legged steed for his riding."

" Get up now," said the nine-legged steed; " get up and shake yourself out of the grass. Go forward. You will find three champions as handsome as ever you saw. Salute them as politely as you can. Tell them you hope they will not be worse than their promise."

He went forward and saluted them. He took them by the hand. He sat in their company till morning. When the day came they were going. They left a breakfast on the table. They gave him the three gifts. They went then and put on the transforming caps. They went away as three seals. The son of the king came down then, and sat under the beast's head.

" Now," said the nine-legged steed, " I have one fault, that a rider never gets on me but I must throw him three times. When you take your breakfast, get a saddle and bridle; put them on me. Take me down to the soft ground ; go riding on me, and I must throw you."

He took his breakfast. He went riding on her then. She asked him if he was ready. He said he was.

"I will throw you as gently and quietly as I can."

She walked a couple of steps. She lifted her rump and flung him. He was jerked up into the air, and fell down on the back of his head.

She came about him. " I believe you are killed."

15

"I am not," said he.   "I am none the worse."

"You are a good man," said she; "if you stand two other tumbles I will never throw you again."

When he was rested, he went riding again. She lifted her rump again, and jerked him into the air. She came about him to see if he was killed.   "I believe you are killed."

"I am none the worse," said he.

"If you stand one more tumble, I will never throw you again."

He rested himself.   He went riding again. She asked him if he was ready.   He said he was. She flung him again and tossed him into the air. He fell down on the back of his head.   She looked about to see if he was alive.   "Now," said she, "I will never throw you again.   Now when you are rested, and you run to your riding, do not pull the bridle on my head.   I know where you are going.   I will bring you to the place you are drawing to."

> She stretched herself to her full speed and red running;
> So that she took the hill at a leap, the glen at a standing jump:
> So that she overtook the wind that was before her,
> And the wind behind did not overtake her:
> Till the cups of her two knees were rubbing her two jaws bare:
> So greatly she was running,

till she came to the door of the king.

"Give me to no one whatever till a red boy comes," said the nine-legged steed.

The king rose out. He gave welcome to the son of the King of Erin. Boys came up to the horse to put her in the stable. He did not give her to them. A red boy came. He asked would he give her to him. She told him to give her. They came into the parlour.

He got dinner then. He was eating and drinking till it was well on in the night. The king said then that he had an island, and that he gained nothing by it for a long time: that Owases were risen up on it.

"I am not going to give my daughter to any one who does not kill them and clear the island."

"We will throw a look around to-morrow," said the son of the King of Erin.

When he took breakfast on the morrow-morning, he went out to the nine-legged steed. She told him what was to be done.

"Put saddle and bridle on me: go riding on me. There are three miles of sea between the land and the island. I will clear the three miles at a leap. Tie me to the stump of a tree."

She went forward then, and he had the ring in his hand. The first Owas man that met him, he raised the ring between himself and him, and blinded him. He was killing and slaughtering till he killed the last on the island. He went down to the nine-legged steed. He went riding on her then, and she cleared the three miles. She told him not to look behind him till he came to the king's door. When he came up to the gate there was thunder and lightning, and he thought the mid-heaven was falling, such was the rattle. There was a great sink of mud at the door of the hen-wife, and when he was going past by the door he looked behind to see if there was anything. He fell into the mud and filth. He got up with dirt and sores on his skin. He was all covered with them.

The daughter of the hen-wife asked leave of her mother to pull him in, or the pigs would tear him. Her mother told her to do it. She pulled him in. She put a wisp of straw under him.

He asked her to go under the window of the greenawn on her two knees. "Ask the girl is there anything at all to do me good, if she hopes to see the man she left behind her at the fountain."

The girl said, "Go into my father's garden. There is a well of fresh water there. There are rushes beside the well. Pull three stalks. Cut the white root. Get a bowl. Raise the full of the bowl out of the well. Rub the white roots in the water until they are melted. Rub the water to his skin. He will be as well as ever he was."

She rubbed the water then on every part of his body. He was as well as he ever was. He had nothing to put on him but old clothes. There was a butler in the great house. He saw the king's son falling. He ran to the place. He took away his clothes. He threw him his own clothes. The king's son had nothing to put on him but the butler's clothes. He went to the house of the king, and he was at work like the butler. The butler was in the king's house in the place of the son of the King of Erin. The king thought it was the son of the King of Erin that was with him. He published word through the island to come to the wedding. The gentlemen were gathered the next day. They went fowling. The king's son was carrying the dogs' food. There came a mist on the hill, and they lost their way. They said they would be lost. The man who was carrying the dogs' food said to the king that if he would give him his daughter in marriage he would save them all till morning. The king said his daughter was given to a gentleman who had come there. The gentlemen then said that they would all be dead in the morning, and it was better for him to tell a lie and to save them.

"Well! I will give you my daughter if you save us," said the king.

He threw down the bag with the dogs' food.

Then he got the apple that he had as a gift. He threw it into the air. Where the apple fell there rose a court and castle. There came food and drink enough for a hundred men. They were hungry, and they ate enough and drank enough. Then they fell asleep. When they woke in the morning, they were lying in a smooth flat of rushes, and they sweating. There was great joy on them. The gentleman then said he should get the woman. When the butler came he had no wife to get. He was vexed. He went home then, and the woman who was in the greenawn said she would not marry a man at all, but the man who would ride the nine-legged steed under the window of the greenawn. The report went out through the island that any man at all who would ride the nine-legged steed, had the king's daughter to get. The people were all gathered. There was a great gathering there. The red boy brought out the nine-legged steed under the windows of the greenawn. The butler would let no one ride till he went riding himself the first time. Then he went riding on her. The nine-legged steed asked him was he ready ; he said he was. She lifted her rump and jerked him up in the air. He fell and was killed. Then there was another rider then and he went riding. She played the same trick with him. She was there, and no one at all was going to ride on her. The king's son

went, and bought himself clothes. He put them
on. He went riding then on the nine-legged
steed. She walked up and down under the
windows of the greenawn, and she stirred not
head nor foot. The lady was looking out of the
window. When she saw him riding, she knew
him and she came down. She ran out and they
caught hold of each other by the hands. There
was great joy on her that she saw him. She
smothered him with kisses, and drowned him with
tears ; she dried him with finest cloths and
with silk.

Came the priest of the pattens and the clerk
of the bells. The pair were married. When they
were married there were three champions there.
They asked him if he knew them. He said that
he knew them ; that it was they gave him the
gifts. There came a beautiful girl then. She
asked him if he knew her. He said he did not
know.

"Well," said she, "I was in the place of the
nine-legged steed, and those are my three brothers,
and I am sister to them. We were all under
spells till your wife was married."

I found the ford ; they the stepping-stones.
They were drowned, and I came away.

THE PHONETIC TEXT.

WHEN folk-lore is narrated by peasants in their own dialect, it seems desirable, for various reasons, that the tales should be recorded in that dialect, and not in some form of speech differing from it more or less widely. This being conceded, the question arises, when one takes to recording Irish folk-lore, how the object is to be attained. It needs but a very small acquaintance with the ordinary Irish orthography to perceive that, if it is adhered to, the object cannot be even aimed at. The greatest defect in the English language is admitted to be its extraordinary spelling. But in this respect it is completely outdone by Irish Gaelic, which is troubled in an aggravated form with every evil that afflicts English. Different sounds are written in the same way. Identical sounds are written in different ways. Silent letters attain to a tropical forestine luxuriance, through which the tongue of the learner despairs of hewing a way. There are, moreover, cases in which there is no indication in writing of single sounds, and even syllables, which are actually pronounced ; and there is at least one case of a word being written as if it began with a vowel, while it really begins with a consonant.

One of the chief reasons for this state of affairs is the attempt which has been made to represent an exceedingly numerous and varied series of sounds with a meagre alphabet of eighteen letters. The system of orthography developed, though highly ingenious, has proved entirely inadequate to its purpose. But if this be true of the so-called classical speech of the few educated persons, whose original pronunciation has been to some slight extent modified by the influence of books, far more decidedly must it be affirmed of the actual peasant dialects which, for two hundred years at least, have taken each of them its own way, uncontrolled by any central influence. Of these the mere sounds cannot be given at all on the basis of the common spelling. Here are two of the simplest examples. The Donegal pronunciation of the word "tá" cannot be written by any device known to Irish orthography ; neither can the Kerry pronunciation of "glean." The strange spectacle is sometimes witnessed of an attempt to give the actual sound of Irish words by means of a spelling based on English values,—of Chaos applying for help to Confusion.

In addition to the reasons which might be urged generally in favour of recording folk-lore in the dialect of the narrators, is one which is largely peculiar to Irish tales. I will indicate it in the briefest manner. Words are of frequent occurrence which are not to be found in the dictionaries. If one of these words contains the sound of *v* or *w*, you cannot tell, if writing in the ordinary way, whether to use *b* or *m* aspirated. If by mistake you choose the wrong letter, you may afterwards throw yourself or others entirely on a wrong scent. But if the actual *v* or *w* is written, you will not be responsible for misleading any one. It is further to be observed that these stories constitute the only body of matter having an intrinsic interest, which can be used as a vehicle for placing some considerable specimens of the spoken language before Continental and other students, who have little opportunity of gaining acquaintance with it directly.

It is true that the difficulties in the way of accurately writing the dialects are formidable. Not only, as already remarked, are the sounds of Irish exceptionally numerous and subtle in any one dialect that may be chosen, but the dialects are well-nigh innumerable. While certain broad differences are characteristic of Kerry, Connaught, and Donegal respectively, there are minor varieties in every district, shading off in every possible

combination into those of the surrounding districts.
The native of Ballymore does not speak as the
inhabitant of Ballybeg, only two miles away ; and
the native of Ballybeg probably has several pro-
nunciations, of which he will give you the benefit
impartially. This last statement must appear
almost incredible, but its truth is unquestionable.
I have taxed the peasants with these variations, and
they have admitted them, only observing " that's
how the word's said there," *i.e.*, in that context.

The alphabet which now follows is the work of
Mr. James Lecky, whose untimely death was a
severe blow to the study of modern Irish. In
addition to the list here given, Mr. Lecky had
noted some additional distinctions, the precise
value of which I do not understand. I have
therefore not employed them in my own stories,
and though I have included one story written
down by himself, I have been obliged to omit
them.

THE ALPHABET.

	PHONETIC SPELLING.	ORDINARY SPELLING.	ENGLISH.
a	maq	mac	son
aa	laa	lá	day
ai	maih	maith	good
aai	faainnje	fáinne	a ring
æ	bæn	bean	a woman
æ"	fæær	feárr	better
e	lesj	leis	with
ee	sjee	sé	he

	PHONETIC SPELLING.	ORDINARY SPELLING.	ENGLISH.
eei	eeisjg	éisg	of a fish
i	min	min	meal
ï or ii	sjï	sí	she
o	qos	cos	foot
oo	boo	bó.	cow
ou	qoul	ca bh-fhuil.	where is?
oi	oiărq.	adharc	a horn
u	muq.	muc	a pig
uu	tuu	tú.	thou

ă, ĕ, ĭ, ŏ, ŭ, are obscure sounds of the ordinary short vowels. ă occurs frequently, the others rarely. i final has the value of y in English " city."

b	baan.	bán	white
d	madu	madadh.	a dog
dj.	djæs.	deas.	pretty
dd	meeădd-sjin	meud-sin	all that *
f	fis	fios	knowledge
fj.	fjuu	fiú	worth
g (slender g)	gæær	geárr	short
c (broad g)	cas	gas	stalk
ç (broad asp.)	mŏ çort.	mŏ ghort	my field
h	huc	thug.	took
hj.	mŏ hjool	mŏ sheól	my sail
j	mŏ jæærher †.	mo dhearbhráthair	my brother
k (slender c)	kool	ceól	music ‡
q (broad c)	qos	cos	foot
x (q asp.)	xirj	chuir.	put §
l	lee	lé	with
lj	balje.	baile.	town
ll	llonc.	long	ship
llj.	lljæbwi	leaba	bed
m	maq.	mac	son
n	noos.	nós	custom
nj.	njïr	nior	neither
nn	bonn.	bonn.	bottom

* Sound hard, as English d.
† Donegal pronunciation.
‡ k asp. = hj.
§ q asp. often = h.

	PHONETIC SPELLING.	ORDINARY SPELLING.	ENGLISH.
nnj	. qrinnju . . .	. cruinniughadh	. assembly
p	. paaisjdje . .	. páisde	. child
r	. rud	. rud	. thing
rj	. erjĕ	. aire	. attention
rr.			
rrj	} see remarks.		
s	. saal	. sál	. heel
sj	. sjæn	. sean	. old
t	. taa	. tá.	. is
tj	. tjïrj	. tír	. country
tt *	. hitt-sjee . .	. thuit-sjee . .	. he fell
v	. mŏ væn. . .	. mŏ bhean . .	. my wife
w	. waru. . . .	. mharbh. . .	. killed

) = a glide.   (iota subscript) is the sign of nasality, mræ̨æ̨.

The most important features in the foregoing
are,—(1) the use of *j*, which when initial has the
German value, to mark slenderness, when attached
to another consonant ; (2) the use of *c* for broad
g, dictated partly by the necessity of economising
the resources of the Roman alphabet, and by the
consideration that *c*, in most alphabets of uncertain
value, and therefore sometimes entirely discarded
by phoneticians, is thereby fixed and utilised ;
(3) the doubling of the vowels, a practice known
in old Irish, to indicate length.   The accents thus
disappear, and, no dots to indicate aspiration being
required, the diacritics, whose number is such a
frequent source of error, are almost entirely got
rid of, the only exception being ◡ the mark of
obscurity, which may be usually omitted without

* Sound hard.

harm, as it never appears except on an unstressed syllable. In the Connaught and Donegal dialects the stress is thrown forward. There are a few exceptions, which are the following : ănsjin, ănsjo, ănoxt, ămæsg, ălig (all), ămax, amwijh, estjæx, estih, ăraan, anisj. All these have the stress on the last syllable, and the final vowel is in every case not obscure. *rr*, written in a few cases, is doubtful. *rrj* corresponding to *llj* and *nnj* does not, I think, occur on the coast of Connaught, and but rarely in Donegal. The *j* is, however, really pronounced as a separate consonant along with the following vowel. Thus, " Tïcerr-je."

The Connaught values of the letters, specially those of Renvyle, are the basis of the alphabet.

APPENDIX.

NĂ TJRÏ MRĄĄ.

Dialect of Renvyle, co. Galway.

Vï aan fær tjïäxt aa hoxrïdj, acăs qasu tjïaxt lee tïu tjæmpăll
ee, qasu doo ql)egăn dine. "S maih ĕ kært çom duurjtt sjee
lesj heen, "ee sjin ă huurjtj ljom acăs ă xirj ăn aatj haa-
waaljtji." Hoog sjee lesj ăn ql)egăn acăs lljæc sjee 's ă
tjæmpăll ee. Çluuăs sjee lesj erj ă vællăx ă walje, acăs qasu
doo fær ăn ourdu din uăsăl. "Kee ră tuu?" duurjtj ă din'
uăsăl. "Vï mee eg soxrïdj ăcăs qasu çom ql)egăn dinĕ er ă
mællăx." "Keerj dă rinnje tuu lesj?" duurjtj ă din' uăsăl.
"Huc mee ljom ăcăs d'aac mee 's ĕ tjæmpăll ee." "Njïr woor
ditj?" duurjtj ă din' uăsăl. "Kee ăn faa sjin?" duurjtj ă fær.
"Bwïĕn ee mă xl)egăn-sĕ" duurjtj ă din' uăsăl, "ăcăs daa
nnjïĕntaa tædi æs bællăx lesj, ça sjuuraaltji veensjĕ suuăs læt."
"Acăs kee ăn xï ăr xaalj tuu dŏ xl(egăn" duurjtj ă fær. "Njïrj
xaalj mee xar ă bih ee, ăx d' aacă mee ins ăn aatj ă wuuerj tis' ee,
ça metts acăm keerd ă jïĕnhaa lesj." "Krjedjim çăr ă dină maih
'uu" duurjtj ă fær ăcăs maa sjææ, b'æær ljom ăn aatj ă kïntjăxt
hele naa ăn dŏ xooloodăr." "Naa bïäx fwatjïs ort. Njï wanj-hă
misje læt. Veeăx foon orăm nïs muu lljæs jïĕnu çwitj naa
doxăr." "Is maih ljom sjin" duurjtj ă fær. Tjænŭitj ă waljĕ
ljomsĕ çă waamidj ĕ nnjïnjeerj." Hjuul sjïäd i-nnjeenjdji ĕ
waljĕ. "Eirji dă hï" duurjtj ă fær lee nă væn, ăcăs faa ăr
nnjïneer ree duunnj. Dj' eirji an væn, acăs fuurj sjï ăn
djïneer ree doofj. Nuurj ă dj ihjidăr ĕ nnjïneer "tjænuetj"
duurjtj ă fær "çă nnjimreemidj qla)efĕ qaarti." Vï sjïĕd ăn
tranhoonă sjin 'g imărjtj xaarti, acăs xodil sjee ăn ïhĕ sjin ins
ĕ tjæx. Acăs erj madjin laarnă waarjăx, dj ihădăr ĕ mrikfwastă
innjeenjdji. Nuurj ĕ vï çaa uurj qatji, "Tjænuitj ljomsĕ" duurjtj

ă din' uăsăl lesj ă vær. " Kee ăn çræhă taa acăd dïumw ? "
duurjtj ĕ fær. "Çă veki tu ăn aatj ă taa acăm 's ă maljĕ."
Dj eerji sjïĕd acăs hjuul sjïĕd innjeenjdji ça nnjæxă sjïĕd că
djï ăn tjæmpăll. " Toog ăn tombw)ă " duurjtj ă din' uăsăl.
D'aardă sjee ăn tombwă ăcăs fuuĕ sjïĕd isjtjax. " Tjeerji sjïs
ăn sdoirje " duurjtj ă din' uăsăl lesj ă vær. Fuuădăr sjïs
innjeendji ça nnjæxi sjïĕd çă djï ăn dorăs, ăcăs hiscliu ee, ăcăs
fuua sjïĕd isjtjæx ça djï ăn hjisjtjinăx. Vï berjtj sjæn-vrąą nă
sïu xosj ne tjinu. "Eeirji " duurjtj ă din' uăsăl lee bæn æqu
acăs faa fwï rjeerj i nnjïneerj duunnj."· Dj'eerji sjï ăcăs huc
sjï lehi fati bĕăcă. Wil acăd çuunnj ça jïneerj ăx ă kinaal
sjin ? " duurjtj ă din' uăsăl : " Njïl " duurjtj ăn væn. " Mar wil
qonnji 'uu heen ïĕd. Eeirji hise " duurjtj sjee lesj ă daarnă
bæn, acăs faa fwï rjeerj i nnjïneerj duunnj." Dj eeirji sjï ăcăs
huc sji lehi min ăcăs qaanhïni lehi. " Nnjænăx wil ăcăd duunnj
ăx ĕ kinaal sjin ? " " Nïl " duurjtj sjï. " Măr bwil qonnji
ee." Fuue sjee suuăs ăn sdoirje ăcăs wuuel sjee ăn dorăs.
Haanik ăn væn vraa ămax ege fwï nă qolhi sjïdă ăcăs ee
ooraaljtji aa voon ă qosje çă djï molăx ĕ kïnnj. Dj ïră sjï
keerd ă vï tæsdaal woi. Dj ïră sjee i veetitt sjï djïneerj aal
çoo heen ăcăs çăn strænsjeere. Duurjtt sjï çă veetăx. Lljæc
sjï djïneer ănuuĕs huqu vï veljuunjtj çă rï.
Acăs nuurj ă vï saa itji ăcăs oolti æqu, dj' ïrhi ăn din' uăsăl
çănnj ær ĕ rou 's ege kee ăn reesuun lee r eed sjï i lljehedj çă
jïneer huurjtj doofj. " Nïl is acăm " duurjtj ăn fær ; ăcas maa
sjee dă hel ee insjï çămw ee. " Nuurj ă vï mee bĕoo, vï mee
poosti tjrï huurje, ăcăs ăn hjeeăd væn vï ăcam, nïrj huc sjï rjïu
çăn woxt ăx fati bĕăcă, acăs qahă sjï hïăxt suuăs hï heen orhu
çă laa 'n vjrjehunisj. An daarnă bæn, nuurj ă dj ïrăx ă dine
boxt djeerjke orhi, nïr huc sjï rjïu doofj ăx min ăcas qaanhïni,
ăcăs nï veei sjï nïs fæær eki heen naa din e bihj hele ïres orhi
ee erjïsjtj, çă laa 'n vjrjehunisj. An tjrïwă bæn lee r ïr mee
'rhi ăn djïneerj aalj fwï rjeerj, dj eeădd sjï sjin xălje hjinaal aa
uus huurjtj duunnj." " Kee ăn faa lee r eedd sjï sjin huurjtj
duunnj ăcăs naar eeăd ăn verjtj el' ee jïenų ? " duurjtj ă fær.
" Măr nnjïr spaaraal sjï rudă bihj daa mĕăx eki rjïu er ă dine
boxt, ăcăs beei ă kinaal sjin eki çă djï laa 'n vjrjehunisj.
Tjænuitj ljom să " duurjtj ă din' uăsăl lesj ă vær çă veki tuu
m' aatju.'"

Vï tjïfwi acăs staabli ăcăs qoilltji tjimpăl ă hï, ăcăs lesj ă
vïrinnjĕ ă jïĕnų vï sjee er in aatj bă djesjĕ henik mee lee mă
çaa huul erjïu. " Tjænuitj ljom sjtjæx insje " duurjtj ă din'
uăsăl lesj ă vær. Njï ră mee wad esjtjihj nuurj ă haanik
pïbwirje ăcăs dj insje sjee er sjinnim hjool : njï· ră sjee wad i
sjinnim nuuirj i lljïĕnų sjtjax ă tjax lee firj ăcăs lee mrąą.
Daati sjïĕd erhu dǫusa. Nuurj ă vï tamwăl çăn ïhje qatji
huuru ljom ʒel ă xolu. Di eerji mee acăs fuue mee ă xolu ăcăs
nuuirj a çuusji mee erj madjin nï ră ænhe erj in aatj er ă tjæx
naa

[The MS. ends here, but there are evidently only two or
three words missing.]

AN ÇLAS CÆVLEN.

Dialect of Achill Island, co. Mayo.

Xuui ă Cobaan Sïăr acăs ă maq sjerj in ă doun sjerj ec Balăr
Beemănn cŏ djaanu quuirtj. " Gerji ăn boohăr, ă vik," ers ăn
tæherj.

Rjih ăn maq ămax rive ăn boohăr, acăs fillj ăn t-æher ă
waljĕ ăn laa sjin. An dæră laa xuui sjiäd erj sjuul, acăs duuertj
ă t-æher lesj ă waq ă boohăr ă jïeru. Rjih sjee ămax rive an
t-æher ăn dæra laa acăs fillj ăn t-æher ă walje. " Kee sjkïăl
çiv ă veeh pillju măr sjin ? " ers ă bæn Cobaain ooig. " Iărĕnn
m'æher orram ăn boohăr iăru : rjih mee ămax an boohăr rive
acăs 'pillen sjee." " Tesji tuu maarăx erj sjgeeăl næx cuuăli
sjee erjïu, acăs misje mani çit-sje næx pilli sjee." Xuui sjeeăd
erj sjuul ăn tjrïwe laa, acăs hesji ăn Cobaan ooc sjgeeăl næx
cooăli ăn t-æher erjïu acăs njïr fill sjee nïs mǫǫ, co djæxi sjiăd
in ă doun herj.

" Nisj," ers ăn væn lee Cobaan ooc, " nææ bï in ăn aatj erjïu
næx mee nă wrąa co moih çitj."

Rjinn sjeeăd ănsjin ăn quuritj co Walăr Beemăn ; acăs njï ră
duul egĕ, ă ligin erj æsj, fwatjïs cŏ njaanitt sjeeăd quuirtj cănj
ær elĕ qoo moih lesj ă quuirtj ă vï egĕ feen.

" Tæærnnjïv woofĕ na stæfŏlj ; " acăs vï duul ă xirj ă maasj ă
maar ă bildaalĕ. Vï qaljïn ă Walăr Beemănn ă col hæært erj
madjin fwï 'n vildal.

" A Cobaain ooig," er sjisje, " xuui erj dŏ xrinaxt : sjïlïm cur

16

fusă sjææxt qloxĕ xahu ănuăs naa ææn kinn ăwaain ă xirj co djï huu." " Is fïr çitj " ers ă Cobaan ooc." Hesji sjïäd ă ligin ănuăs nă hibrje. Nuuirj ă xuuali Balăr Beemănn cŏ ra sjïäd ă xahu ănuăs nă hibrje, d'oordi sjee ăn stæful erjïstj, cur ïsjle sjïäd nă tælŭv. " Nisj ; " ers ăn sjæn Cobaan sïăr " tææ qam in dŏ xidj ibrje ; acăs ă meeu tjrï wall ornesj taa mo jeei 'sa walje acăm, ă ducenn sjïäd qor ăn oiĕ ăn xirj, qam ăn oiĕ ăn xam, acăs bææertj ăn oiĕ nă cancĕdje, acăs njïr eeăn ær lee nă waail ææx dŏ waq feen, jïăroonj ăn obirj acăs njï veeŭv ææn obirj ins a doun ă qompeeraalje leehe. Jofi tuu," er sjesjăn, " bæn eeăn lạav ăwaain ins ă tjæx, acăs paasjdje lljæh-uuil ; acăs qruuăx æruur ins ă dorăs."

Xirj ăn t-æherj lesj llonc ănsjin, acăs xirj sjee næll co h-Eerje ee. Vï sjee erj sjuul erjïu cŏ wuuirj sjee ămax ă tjæx : acăs hænik sjee stjæx in ă tï.

Dj ïări sjee erj, a veeu ăn tjæx Cobaain ooig ? Duuertj ăn væn co mwï ee. " Duuertt sjee ljom cŏ rŏ bæn erj lljæh-lạav, acăs paasjdje lljæh-uuil ins ă tjæx, acăs qruuăx æruur ins ă dorăs." " Næx vekin tuu," er sisjăn, " næx wil acăm æx lljæh-lạav, acăs vekin tuu ăn proosjdje sjŏ erj lạav ă paasjdje ? —nïl is acăm kee ăn moomeedj xirji sjee ăn proosjdje in ă huul acăs a mani sjee ăn tuul ĕs feen ? acăs vekin tuu ăn xruuăx æruur amwihj ins ă dorăs ? "

Dj ïăr sjee ansjin nă tjrï wall. " Kee nă tjrï wall ïad ? " er sjisjăn. " Taa qor ăn oiĕ ăn xirj, qam in oiĕ ăn xæm, acăs bææertj ăn oiĕ nă cancĕdje." Hig sjï ansjin nax ducett sjeeăd erj æsj ă xïe, mar djicett sjï nă foqle-sjŏ.

" Taa nă tjrï wall ins ă xoară sjin hïs, ă ducenn sjïäd, qor ăn oiĕ in xirj, qam in oiĕ ăn xam, acăs bææertj in oiĕ nă cancedje." Xuuă sjï sjïs acăs doscel sjï ăn xoară, acăs duuertt sjï lesj feen ă qromu sjïs co tuunj ă xoară,—cŏ rŏ sji feen ĕnnjisjăl. Xrom sjee sjïs, acăs anuuirj fuuirj sjï qrom ee, xa sjï stjæx ins ă xoor' ee, acăs çridj sjï ăn xoară erj, acăs duuertt sjï lesj co wanitt sjee ansjin co djicu Cobaan ooc acăs sjæn Cobaan ă walje, acăs luuăx ă sïhirj, Xor sjï qontăs ec Balăr Beemăn co ro waq a *confinement,* eki co dj icu Cobaan ooc acăs sjæn Cobaan a walje. Xor sjee lljoofwe llonc acăs xirj sjee a walj ïad feen acăs ă paaiĕ ; acăs lig sjisje maq Walăr Beemann erj æsj egesăn. Nuuirj ă vï sjïäd ec imæxt ă walje,

dj ïäri Balăr Beemăn cŏ Cobaan, kee ăn gouĕ jofitt sjee ă xirju
ïărĕnaxă lee hï ăn xuuirtj. " Nïl eeăn gou' in Eerinn is fæær
næææ Cavidjïn Coo." Nuuirj ă hænik sjæn Cobaan ă walje
duuĕrtt sjee lee Cavidjïn Coo căn eeăn paai erj bih ă claqu
wuui, erj ïărenaxă ă jaanu con quuirtj, æææx ă çlas :—çaa curti
fuuiĕ fïhje barillje co lïnitt sjï lee bannjĕ nă fïhje barillje.

Sjkrïu ansjin Balăr Beemăn co djï an Cavidjïn Coo, co dooritt
sjee çoo ăn çlas, æææx ă ïĕrănaxa ă jaanu con quuirtj : æææx njï
huc sjee ăn wuuĕrăx çoo nuuirj ă xirj sjee egĕ ăn çlăs ; acăs vïs
egĕ co nnjimoott sjï wuuă, nuuirj næx duc sjee çoo ăn wuuĕrăx.

Sjee ăn marăcu jaanitt Cavidjïn Coo ănsjin lee hole Cæsjkiăx
ă hicu ege ;—æn çlas ærje acăs ă hoort egĕ slaan ă walje ă
trænoona ; jaanitt sjee qlæve cŏ holĕ cæsjkiăx ă dj ærju ï. Dj
ïsitt sjï feeŭr Qruuăxaan Qonăxtă ăn laa, acăs d' oolitt sjï djox ă
Lax Eeăxirj ă Cuuicălu ă trænoona.

Hænig Kiăn waq Qaantje egĕ, cŏ waadd sjee qlave djaanti.
Duuert sjee lesj cŏ nnjaanu, æææx cur ă bee ă warăcu ă vee egĕ,
co coihitt sjee ăn çlas ærje ăn laa sjin. " Næ măr rŏ sjï læt ă
walje acăm trænoona, qoihi tuu do hjinn ă ligin sjïs erj anj
ïnuur co mani mee an kinn jiĕt, lee do xlave feen."

Dj imi Kïan waq Qaantje acăs ruc sjee grjim robel orhi.
Nuuirj ă hænik sjee ă walje trænoonă, " Sjo ï, mwihj, ă çlas "
er sjesjăn lee Cavidjïn Cou. Vï Cæsjkiăx esti ins ă hjææærtă,
Ridjirje ăn çaairje. Rjih sjee ămax, acăs duuĕrtt sjee lee Kïan
waq Qaantje, " tæææ 'n cou ă xirj ăn ouĕrtj in dŏ xlave, acăs măr
rŏ grjim acăd erj njï bee buui imăru acăd." Nuuirj ă xuui Kïan
waq Qaantje estjæx njï q)ivne sjee ăn çlas ă xirj estjæx. Dj
ïäri Cavidjïn Cou çe " Kee wil ăn çlas ? " " Sjo ï amwihj ec
an doras ï." " Xirj estjæx ï " er sjesjăn. Nuuirj ă xuui sjee
amax, vï sjï imi. " Lig sjïs do hjinn erj ănj ïnuur, co mani
mee ăn konn diĕt." " Tæææ mee ïäri onoorj hjrï laa ort lee
col ă hïäri." " Veerhi mee sjin ditj " er sjesjan.

Dj imi sjee lesj ansjin acas vï sjee lljænuintj ă lorăc co dænik
sjee co djï ăn ærige. Vï sjee sjïr acăs enjïär erj ă traai, dæææ
tærentj ă cruuĕgĕ daa xlæcenn lee buuĕrhe enjeei nă clasjĕ.
Vï fær amwihj erj ăn ærige in ă xorăx. Dj omirj sjee estjæx co
djï ee, acas vï ăn fær sjin Mananaan bwï maq ă Ljirj. Dj ïäri
sjee çe " Kee ă taa ort ennju ? " Dj ini sjee çoo. " Keeărd ă
veerhaa con tjie d' aaqu huu ins ăn aatj ă wil ăn çlas ? " " Nïl

dædi acăm lee toortj çoo." " Njïr iări mee ort æææx lljæh ă
ncruui tuu co djige tuu erj æsj." " Veerhi mee sjin ditj " ers ă
Kïăn waq Qaantje. " Bï 's estjih ins ă xorăx." Lee locen do
huul, d' aac sjee ee herj ă riaxtă nă fuuăriaxt ; njïr brjïhu eeăn
grjim erjïu erj ăn ilaan-sjŏ, æææx djih sjïăd ă hole hoort bï
fuuăr. Rjinn Kïăn waq Qaantje tjini, acăs hesji sjæ brjïh ăn
vï. Nuuirj ă xuăli Balăr Beemănn co rŏ lehidj onn, hooc sjee
estjæx na qookerje, acăs nă sjgeeăli, acăs ănj ær tjini ee.
Well ; vï æææn ïen ăwaain ec Balăr Beemann acăs rjinnju
tariceræææxt cur bee ăn maq eki ă warahu ăn t-æherj woor.
Xoi sjee ănsjin in ă *confinement* ï, fwatjïs co ræhi anj ær dæææ
xooirj, acăs ee feen ă veeuv lee vïa eki ; acăs sjee ăn *companion*
eki, *dummy* mraạ. D'aac Mananaan buui co Kïan waq Qaantje
—clas erj bih ă luqett sjee laạu erj fwosceltj acăs dridj nă jeei.
Vï sjee c' ouărq erj Balăr Beemann ă çol co djï ăn tjæx-sjo donnj
ïen lee bïa eki ; acăs xuuă 'sjee feen nă jeei co djï ăn tjæx ;
acăs loc sjæ laạu erj ăn clas, acăs doscĕl ăn dorăs ; njï wuuirj
sjee æx ăn vertj wan onn. Rjinn sjee tjinni çoofwe. Vï sjee
tjæææxt onn erjïu, cur qasu dinĕ qlanne orhi. Vï sjee col ec
imæææxt ansjin nuuirj ă rucu ă paasjdje. Xuuă sjee cŏ djï ăn
rjï acăs duuĕrtt sjee lesj cŏ coihitt sjee imæxt. " Tige n imæhă ? "
er sjesjăn. " Taa, djeerji mælhoo çam oo hænik mee in ăn
ilaan-sjo. Qoihi mee imæxt." " Kee an mælhu ee ? " er sjesjan.
" Qasu dine xlanne orrăm."

Vï bertj waq çoo erj ăn ilaan elĕ fjoolăm drïaxta. Hænik
sjïăd ă waljĕ erj xuuirtj ec ăn æherj. " Æherj " ers ă fær aqu,
xirji dŏ sjgeeăli, dŏ qookerjĕ acăs d' ær tjinu dŏ haai feric ort."
Vï Kïăn waq Qaantje c eesjtjæxt çaa ræææitj, xuuă sjee cŏ djï ăn
ïen Walăr Beemann, acăs dj' ini sjee ăn sjgeeăl dih ă d'inisj ă
drïhaar. " *Well !* " er sjisje, " taa sjee ăn am acăd ă veeh
c'imæææxt anisj. Sjin ï, qruuăxt erj ă walle, buuărax ăn clasje,
acăs beei ăn çlas xoo luuă læt ; acăs toor læt ăn paasjdje." Dj
imi sjee acăs ănuuirj ă hænik sjee co djï ăn *spot* ă xirj
Mananaan ămax ee vï Mananaan onn erj ă *spot.* " Bï estih ins
a xoræx " ers ă Mananaan ; "acăs djaan djefirj, næææ baaihi
Balăr Beemann sjinn maa hig lesj ee ; æææx is muu ăn drïăxtă
taa acamsă naa ege," ers ă Mananaan Bwï waq ă Ljirj. Lljeem
sjee estjæx ins ă xorăx acăs lljeem ăn çlas estjæx xoo lluuă lesj.
Lljæn Balăr Beemann ïăd, acăs hooc sjee ăn ærige in ă stirm,

rive acăs nă jeei : njï rjinn Mananaan æææx ă lạau ă hïnu amax
acăs rjinn sjee ăn ærige kuun. Lljæs Balăr ăn ærige rive, duul lee
co nuuihitt sjee iäd ; æææx xoih Mananaan amax qlox acăs xirj
sjee es ăn ærige.

" Nisj, ă Hhjïan waq Qaantje, tææ tuu slaan, saawalti ins ă
walje ; acăs keeărd ă verhis tuu ljom erj ă hon ? "

" Njïl dædi acăm lee toortj ditj æææx ă paasjdje acăs njï
rææhimwidj ă djaanu çaa llje çe, æææx verhim çitj ĕlig ee."

" Tææ mee bwiäx ditj : sjin ee ăn rud ă vï mee iäri.
Njï veei eeăn cæsjkiăx ins ă doun qoo maih lesj," ers ă
Mananaan.

Hooc sjee suuăs lee klæs luu acăs cæsjqu ee. Sjee ăn tænim
ă waasjtje Mananaan erj, ă Doll Daana. Vï sjee acăs Mananaan laa amwihj erj ăn ærige, acăs hænik sjiäd *fleet* Walăr
Beemănn ă sjoolu.

Xirj Doll Daană faainnje, erj a huul, acăs hænik sjee ăn
t-æher moor erj ă *deck*, a spasjdooræxt. Njï rou 's ege cur
bee ee ăn t-æher moor. Losjk sjee lesj *dart* es ă fooqă acăs
warĕ sjĕe ee. Vï ăn tærăcerææxt *fulfil*-aaltji ănsjin.

BRJEEĂXT ĂN DOONJ.

Dialect of Glencolumkille, co. Donegal.

Vï rjï ănsjin acăs njï roo egĕ æx ăn maq ăwaain. Vï sjee 'mwih
ă sjelig. Vï sjee col hææært nă relig. Vï kærher ins ă relig acăs
qorp aqu. Vï feeăx erj ă xorp. Xuui maq rjï estjæx. Dj' esă
sjee cŏdjee vï orhu. Ers ă fær " Tææ feeăxă oinnjĕ erj ănj 'ær
ă tææ maru. Nïl mee sææsta qorp ă xor, cŏ nnjææli çææ waq
tææ ănsjŏ cŏ nnjïŏli sjeeăd nă feeăxă." " Nïl sjinn æææbŭlt ă
nnjïŏl " ers ă fær aqu." " Tææ quuig font oimsă " ers ă maq ă
rjï. " Veerhi mee çïv ee erj ă qorp ă xor." Huc sjee çooif na
quuig font. Qwirju ăn qorp. Dj 'imi maq ă rjï nă helig. Xuuă
sjee ă walje trænoonă. Madjin laar nă waarăx vï sjnæææxt ann.
Xuuă sjee ămax ă helig erj ă tjrææxtă. Warĕ sjee prjeeăxaan
duh. Hæs sjee nă hjonn acăs d' ouĕr sjee erj. Duur sjee n
intjin heen næææx boositt sjee væn ă xiĕ æx ă væn ă meeu ă
kinn qoo duh lee kletj anj eein, noo qrækonn qoo gæl lesj ă
tjræææxtă, gruuie qoo djærăc lesj ăn il. Hæne sjee ă walje.
Laarnă waarăx nuuirj ă dj eerji sjee njï sjee heen acăs dj imi

sjee lesj cŏ waadd sjee ăn væn-sjo. Nuuirj ă vï sjee sjuul lesj
tæmăl, qæsu buuăxoll ruuă doo. Væni ă buuăxŏll doo. Dj esă
sjee qææd ă vï sjee col. Dj inisj maq ă rjï doo çŏ ră sjee col cŏ
vekitt sjee ăn ouĕrq ăwaain erj ă væn sjin. "'S fæær misj'
æsdoo" ers a buuăxol ruuă : " Codjee ăn tuu-ărăsdăl vees tuu
iări ?" " Lljæh ă sïræhæmwidj konn laa acăs bliĕn." Hjuul ă
vertj lljoofwĕ cŏ roo 'n træænoon' ann. Ers ăn fær ruuă " tææ
fær mwintjĕræx duusă nă xooni 's ă xillj-sjŏ hïs. Fan his' ănsjŏ
cŏ dj ige misje nïs." Xuui ăn fær ruuă sjïs cŏ tjæx ăn æhi. Vï
ăn faahăx nă hïe erj qahirj ec ăn tjini. " Onkĕl jïlisj" ers ăn
fær ruuă " mar sjoo tææ tuu ?" " Sjææ çine wintjerje jïlisj ;
cŏdjee tææ tjææxt orrăm ?"
Ers ăn fær ruuă " Rjï ăn Doon hirj woor-wantjrææt tjææxt
nuuăs ănsjin lee dŏ waruĕ. Coo ă walăx ă hileshuu." (?) " Tææ
tjææx ïĕrennj oim mwïh ănsjŏ. Clasæ̈æl mee stjæx ann."
Clasæ̈æl sjee ăn fær estjæx. Xuuă sjee insjerj ă woisjter. Huc
sjee ă woisjter huuas cŏ tjæx ăn æhi. Rinn sjee roi ă supæær.
Xuuă sjeeăd ă llïĕ.
Sjee ăn jeemnæx vï ec ăn æhăx erj madjin " Woscel iăd."
Xuui ă fær ruuă insjerj. Dj esă sjee cŏdjee vï erj?" " Tææ
mee xooirj ă veeh reei lesj ăn oqrăs. Lig ămax es sjo mee
klisju." (?) " Njï liki mee 'max huu" ers ă fær ruuă co nj insji
tuu duh qou'l ă qlooxă dorăxă." " Sjin ₍rud næx n' insji mee
don 'ine cŏ brææ." " *Well !* maa's fæær lät cän insje noo veeh
ănsjin co waa tuu baas."
" Ol ă ră mee nïs fwidj ann, tææ sjee qroxt in ă lljeehidd-sjŏ
room."
" Tææ 's oimsă" ers ă fær ruuă, " qou'l sjee ; bï hise ănsjin
ætts tol lät." Nuuirj ă xooli ăn fahax næx wïtt sjee ămax, huc
sjee lljeem 'max edjirj çææ ronqă don tjæx iărenj. Rinnju çææ
lljeh doo. Hitj lljæh ămwih acăs lljæh estih. Xuui ă fær ruuă
cŏ tjæx ăn æhi. Rinn sjee reei ă mrikwast. Huc sjee lljoofwe
nnjært ooirj acăs ærigidj ;—çææ jæræn acas çææ jiŏlledj. Dj
imi sjeeăd lljoofwe co ro 'n trænoon' ann, co d'æni sjeeăd
estjæx ă collj elĕ.

[In this wood is another giant, from whom in the same fashion
he obtains the " broocă sjlouănă" ; and then they go on to
another wood, in which is another giant, from whom they obtain
the " qelev solaste."]

"' Nisj " ers an fær ruuă, lee nă woisjter " bïmwidj ă tjæxt ă welje : tææ ăr sææih oinnj. Nææ coo ăn tasi nïs fwidje. Væn ă wil tuu tærentj orhi—nïl æn xrænn ins ă xollj næx wil konn dine qroxt erj, æx æn qrænn ăwaain tææ fwirjææxt lee dŏ hjonn-să. Pilamwidj ă walje " ers ă fær ruuă. " Njï rææhe mee ă walje xïĕ " ers ă maq ă rjï " co veki mee 'n ouĕrq ăwaain erj ă væn sjin."

Xo sjeeăd ăn tasi co djæhi sjæd (co) tjæx ă rjï. Rinn ăn rjï fwaruætje woor rive. Claq sjeeăd ăn ïneerj. Xa sjeeăd ăn ïh ec ool acăs lee *sport*. Nuuirj ă vï sjïăd nă sïĕ ec nă supæær hæne sjisj ănuuăs ă tjæx baar. Vï ăn konn qoo duh lee etje ănj eein, qrækon qoo gæl lesj ă tjrææxtă acăs cruuïe qoo djærăc lesj ăn il. Hæne sjï æd lljoofwe 'n ææitj ă ră sjeeăd ec ïhĕ. Xa sjï qïăr insjerj. Duur sjï lesj mar meeu qïărsăn egĕ lee toortj dih maarăx co mwinett sjï ăn konn dih. Ruc sjee erj ă xïăr. Xor sjee sjïs in ă fooq'i. Nuuirj ă vï sjeeăd ă col ă llïĕ, ers ăn fær ruuă lesj " ouărq ă wil ă xïăr oiăd." Xor sjee veeur in ă fooqă.

Njï ro ăn xïăr ege. Hilh nă djooră. " Truuă nær ă (c)laqĕ mee dŏ xoorlje, nuuirj a dj ïăr tuu orram pillju welje." " Beedjirj co wïmisj buui ălig erj " ers ă fær ruuă." Vï sjee ă vlandăr cŏ wuuirj sjee co llï ee. Nuuirj ă xirj ă fær ruuă ă llï ee xor sjee erj ă qlooxă dorraxă. Huc sjee lesj nă broocă sjlouănă, acăs ă qelĕv salăstĕ. Xo sjee ămax acăs hæs sjee 's ă *wack-yard*. Hæne sjisj' amax. Rinn sjï sjïs erj ăn ærige. Hæne sjï æd lesj ăn ærigĕ. Xa sjï blïăsq es ă fooqă. Rinn sjï baad dih. Xo sjï stjæx s ă waad. Wuuil sjï 'c imăru lee cææ fædĕl, co d'æne sjï sjtjæx erj ăn ilææn vï ins ăn ærige. Vï fæhăx moor erj ă xladăx. " Wil dædi læt huum ănoxt ? " " Nïl " er sjisje, " æx beei sjee 's ăn ïh maarăx ljom. Tææ maq rjï Eerinnĕ 'noxt oim. Beei sjee ljom insj' ortsă maarăx."

Xuuă sjeeăd nă tïă ; " Sjoudj qïăr huc misje çoosăn noxt. Tææ sjï hisï." D'æscel ă fæhax qooră. D' aac sjee ăn xïăr erj hoonj ă xooră. Vï ăn fær ruuă ă hæsu erj konn nă xooră. Nuuirj ă d' aac ăn faahăx ăn xïăr ins ă xooră ruc ă fær ruu' orhi nuu cur xŏ sjee nă fooq'ï. Vï ăn tjæx laan cooirj. Xŏ sjï blïe nă ncooirj cur vlï sjï tjrïăn muunj acăs folĕ. Rinn sjï reei ă supæær. Claq sjeeăd ă *stuff* sjin. Hærnă fahăx ege kleeŏrsi ïarĕnnj acăs qrækon laarje baannje. Llï sjeeăd ansjin cŏ madjin.

Nuuirj ă hænik ăn laa, dj eerji sjisje acăs dj imi sjï tærentj erj ăn ærigĕ. Lljæn ă fær ruua ï. Nuuirj ă xŏ sjï æd lesj ă waad xor sjï ăn baad erj ăn isjgĕ. Xuuă sjï heen estjæx inti. Lljæn ă fær ruua ï erj ăn ærige. Vï sjee sjkeetææl insj' orhi lesj ă qlev salăstă. Njï roo 's egĕ codjee vï ă flehu. Nuuirj ă xo sjïăd æd lesj ă walje xuui ă fær ruuă insjerj ă woisjter. Dj esi sjee ră sjee nă xollu. Duurtj maq ă rjï næx roo. "Hææwăl misje dŏ hjonn ănoxt. Sjoudj ă xïr. Qwirj in dŏ fooq' ï." Xor sjee ăn xïr in ă fooqă. Xuui ăn fær ruuă ă llïe. Nuuirj ă vï ăn brikwastă reei erj madjin *ring*-ææl ăn *bell.* Dj eerji sjeeăd acăs njï sjeeăd iăd heen. Nuuirj ă vï sjeeăd claqu mrikwastă hæni sjisj' ănuuăs ăn tjæx baar. "Wil ă xïr oiăd huc misj ĕreeirj?" Xor sjee veer in ă fooqă. Xă sjee ăn xïr insj orhi. Nuuirj ă hæne sjï co roo ăn xïr lee faail egĕ, hæne sjï hææert lee *sweep* awaain. Vrjisj sjï lljæh ă vï erj ă taabĕlĕ. "Tææ tjrïăn don ïne bontj oiăm" ers ă maq rjï Eerinne. "Tææ" ers ăn rjï. "'S tuu ăn cæsjkiăx is fæær ă hænik in mŏ hï erjïu."

Xo sjeeăd ă helig ăn laa sjin. Nuuirj ă hæni sjeeăd a walje vï sjeeăd djænu grinn acas qodjæætă cŏ d'ænik æm supæærĕ. Nuuirj a vï sjeeăd claqu supæær hænik ă væn vrjee æd lljoofwe. Xa sji sjisuur insjerj. "Mar roo'sj oiăd lee toortj duuh maarăx beei dŏ hjonn oiăm." Ruc sjee erj a tj-isuur. Xirj sjee na fooq ee. Nuuirj ă vï sjeeăd ă col ă llïĕ "ouĕrq" ers ă fær ruuă lee na woisjter "wil ă sjisuur oiăd." "Nïl" ers ă moisjter. "S dæn ă halj tuu ee." Xo sjee ă x)ïnu. Vï 'n fær ruuă ă vlandăr cŏ wuuirj sjee llï ee. Nuuirj ă xollĕ sjee, xuui ă fær ruuă ămax. Xor sjee erj ă qlooxă dorrăxă acăs nă Broocă sjlouĕnĕ, acăs huc sjee qelev salăste.

[The visit to the giant in the island is repeated, the red man bringing back the scissors as the comb.]

Nuuirj ă vï an brikwasta reei hæne sjï nuuăs ăn tjæx waar. Vï sjï flox, baaitjï. Djesă sjï dih ro 'n sjisuur ege lee toortj dïh. Xor sjee ă veer in ă fooqă, xa sjee insj' orhi ăn sjisuur. Huc sjï ăn *sweep* awaain, njïr aac sjï grim *delf* erj ă taabele nær vrjisj sjï lee mïhæsu. Duurtj maq ă rjï cŏ roo çææ djrïĕn ăn ïnĕ bontj enjuh egĕ. "Tææ" ers ă rjï "acăs tææ huul oiăm co mwinĕ tuu' lig ï : tææ misje torsaail lehi."

Xa sjeeăd ă laa sjin ă sjelig, cŏ d'ænik ăn ïhĕ. Nuuirj ă vï ă

supæær reei, hæne sjisj' anuuăs lee *flight.* "Mar roo nă
pushini djerinææhă fooqăs misj' anoxt, beei dŏ hjonn oiăm."
"S deli duusă" ers ă maq ă rjï, "fis ă veeh oimsă codjee nă
pushini djerinææhă fooqăs tise." Vï sjee cŏ buuerhĕ næx roos
ege codjee jæænitt sjee. Vï 'n fær ruuă dæ vlandăr cŏ wuuirj
sjee nă llï ee.

[The red man goes with the cloak, &c., as before, and follows
her to the island.]

Nuuirj ă xo sjï ă djirj erj ăn ilææn, vï ăn fahăx ă buuĕrfi erj
ă xladăx. "Wil dædi læt insj' orram?" ers ăn fahăx. "Njï
huuri mee ăn dæh xï insj ort. Lig tuu erj sjuul ă xïr. Lig tuu
erj sjuul ă sjisuur. Vï ăn dææ qidj egĕ lee toort duuh erj
madjin. Xirj misje gæs anoxt erj næx mïĕn egĕ lee toortj duuh.
Sjin ï nă pusjini djerinææha fookinj ănoxt acăs sjin hisĕ."

Xo sjï nă vlïĕ nă ncooirj. Wuun tjrïĕn fală acăs tjrïĕn muunj.
Rinn sjï reei nă hupæære. Dj ïh sjeeăd acăs ool sjeeăd ă
sææih doo. Fuuirj sjee qleeŏrsă iărenj, qrækon laairje baannje.
Llï sjeeăd ansjin co madjin. Nuuirj ă hænik ăn laa laarnă waarăx
fooc sjisje tjrï h-uuirje. "Sjin ï nă pusjini djerinææhă fooqas
misje. Njï veei sjeeăd sjin egĕ lee toort ditj maarăx."

Dj eerji sjï acăs dj imi sjï. Nuuirj ă xo sjï 'max, sjgib ă fær
ruuă konn don æhăx. Xor sjee gæd in ă xluĕsj. Xa sjee erj ă
çooălenj ee. Vï sjee erj ă xladăx qoo luuă leehi-sje. Xo sjisj
estjæx 's ă waad. Vï sjï tærentj erj ă walje. Xo sjesjăn amax
na djeei. Erj veeăd ă lljox sjee ï nă hïhe hele lljox sjee çææ
huuirj qoo moor ăn ïhĕ sjĕ. Xuuă sjeeăd ă walje. Xuui ă fær
ruuă 'n ææitj ă roo 'n moisjter ă llïĕ. "Will tuu dŏ xollu, ă
woisjter?" "Nil mee anisj" ers ă maq ă rjï. "Sjoudj nă
pusjini djerinææhă fooc sjisj nă reeirj, acăs, lljooca, ba cræænă
nă pusjini iad ec *lady* ă veeh boocu." Ruc sjee erj ă konn acăs
xa sjee fwï 'n lljæbwi ee. Nuuirj ă vï 'n brikwasta reei erj
madjin hæne sjisj' ănuuăs lee *flight.* Djesă sjï çih "qoul nă
pusjini djerinææhă fooc misj ĕreejrj?" Xor sjee lạau hærisj fwï
'n lljæbwi. Ruc sjee ăn konn ăn æhi. Xa sjee 'nonns nă qasi.
Nuuirj ă hæne sjisje cŏ roo faahax maru, huc sjï *sweep* awaain ;
njïr aac sjï taabĕl noo qahirj, noo dædi ă roo erj ă taabele næx
djær sjï smolocă dih, vï sjï qoo mïhæstă. "Tææ do nïn ălig
buntj oiăm" ers ă maq ă rjï. "Tææ: acăs is tuu ăn cæsjkiăx
's fæær ă hænik foo mŏ hæx erjïu."

"*Well!* ræhæmwidj ă helig enjuh" ers ăn fær ruuă. Xuuă sjeeăd ă helig. Win ăn fær ruuă tjrï buĕltjïn. Rinn sjee tjrï huusjtĕ. Nuuirj ă xŏ sjeeăd ă walje "nisj" ers ă fær ruuă, "tuurj amax do nïn ănsjo." Huc ă rjï ămax ï. "Kæncel ă qos acăs ă ląąwe" ers a fær ruua: "faac na llï ănsjo ï." D'aac ă rjï nă llï ï. Huc ăn fær ruuă suustje don rjï acăs konn dŏ woisjter. "Buuil hise ăn hjeeăd wullje." Wuuil ă rjï ăn hjeeăd wullje. Vï ăn tjruur ă buuĕlu erj feg tæmăl fadă. Djimï bloirje tjinu 'max æs ă beeăl. "Buuelici liv tjilu. Tææ tjilu intji." Wuuil sjeeăd lljoofwe cur imi kræp elĕ tjinu 'max æs ă beeăl. "Buuĕlici lif" ers ă fær ruuă. "Tææ konn elĕ intji?" Wuuel sjeeăd lljoofwe cur imi ăn tjrïwe konn. "Nææ buuelici nïs mǫǫ" ers ăn fær ruua. "Sjin tjrï jïăwăl djimi esjtje. Scïlici ï 'nisj. Tææ sjï qoo saqirj lee æn væn erj a walje." Scïl sjeeăd ï acăs xor sjeeăd ă llï ï. Vï sjï torsaax ă njeei ă buuelu.

Fuui ă soiert meesje acăs kleerjăx qloihje. Poosu 'n laanawin. D'æn ă fær ruua aqu laa acas blïĕn. Ruucu maq ooc çooif. Nuuirj ă vï ăn laa acăs blïĕn 'stih duuertj ă fær ruua—cur vïhidj lesj ă veeh 'c imææxt. "Nïl is oims" ers ă maq ă rjï cŏdjee jæænhăs misje dŏ jeei." "Oh! njï vee mwillj ort" ers ă fær ruuă; "is qooirj ăn saqru." "S qooirj." ers a maq ă rjï. Xoo (?) sjee çææ lljeh dææ wuuirj sjee ă d'æsdoo sjee ee." "Veerhi mee ăn paaisjdje ălig 'itj" ers ă maq ă rjï: "tææ truui orm ă col ă jæru." "Njï claqi mee ălig ee" ers ă fær ruuă: "njï claqi mee æx mo warăcă." Ruc maq a rjï erj ă sjgon (? sjgian) col a jæru. "*Stop* dŏ laau" ers ă fær ruuă. "Vï tuu heen fuuăscoltjæx. A qiminæx læt ă laa vï tuu col hært lesj ă relig. Vï kærherj ins ă relig acăs qorp ooqu, acăs ïăd ec ærigæl. Vï feeăx erj a xorp. Njï roo sjeeăd sææstă ă xorp ă xor co nnjïălti nă feeăxă. Vï quuig font oïădsă. Huc tuu çooif ee ă xorp a xor. Misje vï 's ă xooră ăn laa sjin. Nuuirj ă hæne misje hise col ă konn ă *journey* hænik misj insj ort lee do hææwăl, măr vï tuu heen qoo moih sjin. Pronam do faaisjdj' ort acăs dŏ xidj ærigidj. Slaan acăs bænææt oïăd. Njï eki tuu æn ouărq orramsă nïs mǫǫ."

[*Note.*—English words or parts of words retaining their pronunciation are in italics.]

NOTES.

The spelling of the names in the English is English phonetic, with the exception of the use of J to denote slenderness or softness of the consonant. English readers are now familiar with a similar use of J in the Norwegian name Björnsen. It is equivalent to the consonantal use of English y.

PAGE 1. The "Gloss Gavlen" means simply the Grey (cow) of the Smith, gavlen being properly gavnen—(gaibh-nenn) according to O'Donovan. The first part of the story has no real connection with the second. The Gobaun seer, meaning the Smith-builder, was the famous mythic architect, to whom was attributed the erection of various actual edifices,—of which I can only recall at present the Round Tower of Killala. The latter part of the narrative is a genuine folk-reminiscence of some of the most striking characters and events in the oldest Irish mythology. Balar of the Blows (Bemann) was the leader of the Fohmors, the powers of darkness and evil, in the great battle of the northern Moytura, fought near Sligo, in which they were defeated by Lugh, Balar's daughter's son, also called Ildauna—that is "of all arts and sciences," the Irish Apollo, or culture-hero. Of this name, the appellation of Dul Dauna, the Blind-Stubborn, here bestowed on him, appears to be a curious corruption. It is interesting to compare the whole of this account with that found by O'Donovan in Donegal. (See note to Annals of the Four Masters—year of the world 3330.) It contains no reference to the education by Mananaun Mac Lir, the sea-god. It represents the Gloss as originally the property of the smith, Gavida, which appears to be correct.

Page 5. "Cruahaun of Connaught," in the modern county of Roscommon, being separated from the nearest part of Ulster by the county of Leitrim, we gain an idea of what a formidable task it was to herd the Gloss. There is no mention of Ulster in the Irish version, but McGinty told me the lake was in that province.

Page 6. "The Kingdoms of the Cold." This indicates a different geography from that of the opening, in which Balar is located in the East. It seems to identify Balar with the powers of the cold. For a full development of this idea, see the writer's poem "Moytura," in "Fand and Other Poems."

Page 10. "Morraha." The title is curious. Binn Edin has not been identified (it can hardly be Binn Eadar, Howth), though the mention at the end of "Bioultach" places it on the coast. It occurs in other tales, Connal Gulban for example, and it seems to be famous in this kind of literature. The present tale has, so far as I know, only one printed variant, the "Fis fá an aon Sgeul" of Kennedy, not so interesting, I think, as this. The story having two parts, I have ventured to give the best version of each from two different narrators. Substantially both are alike throughout. In the Renvyle version of the opening, the hero is Brian Boru, the victor of Clontarf, and the enchanter is named Flauheen O'Neill. The woman is Flauheen's wife. The tone is prosy, all the picturesque incidents relating to the horse being absent. The "story," however, is better told than in the Achill version, except as regards one point, which supplies the wife's motive for treating her husband as she did. He had found in the woods a wild-man (geltj), whom he took into his house, cleaned and shaved, and made a servant of. This man became his wife's lover, and on his detecting the fact, she struck him with a rod of druidism, turning him first into a kitchen block, continually kicked and maltreated. I should have stated in the text that the brief conversation preceding the "story" is from the Achill version. Anshgay-liacht, the name of the one-eyed monster who stole the children, was the brother of the champion who came in the currach. This name is strange, as it is simply an sjgeeliaxt —*i.e.,* "the story telling." In the Renvyle version of the conclusion, the hero baffles the enchanter, by pretending to notice some writing on the sword after he has given it to Flauheen. The latter could not read, and gives it back to the other, who immediately cuts his head off. The Achill pretext for not giving the sword up at all,—"though I promised to bring it as far as you, I did not promise to bring it for you,"—is a favourite device in the island. It will be found again in "King Mananaun," and twice in "The King who had Twelve Sons."

The word translated "thistles" is snæhĕdi, which usually means needles. The narrator said it meant thistles here.

Page 14. The bells rang : cf.,

> " And when in Salamanca's cave
> Him listed his magic wand to wave,
> The bells would ring in Notre Dame."

Page 15. Diversion. The word was so pronounced—not div*a*rsion.

Page 31. "The Ghost and his Wives." The word translated churchyard usually means "church" only.

Page 35. I know of no parallel to this story as a whole. "Bioultach" probably means "Yellow-hair"—"bwï-oltax." Is he a solar hero? There is true painting of certain sides of Irish character in this tale ; the mutual affection of the brothers, their indifference to larger interests, must be noted.

Page 50. This sea-run is a fairly good specimen of this style of composition. There are several words I am unable to translate. As regards the style of the runs in general in Celtic tales, I am unable to accept the view that it has anything in common with the well-known corrupt literary Irish style. There is this fundamental difference between the two. The bombast and exaggeration of the written literature is seriously given, seriously meant. In the "runs" of the oral literature the whole description is obviously fantastic, and meant for such. Popular taste would never have endured the laboured exaggeration which the pedantry of half-educated scribe composers thought so fine ; nor would the outrageous accumulation of alliterative adjectives, in which such persons indulged, have been possible of invention by oral reciters on the spur of the moment. The first of the runs here given shows, by the unintelligibility of part of it, that the narrator was not inventing, but merely giving an imperfect version to the best of his ability. He did not know the meaning of half of it. I now add the Irish of this run, and for the purposes of comparison two others :—

" Hoog sjïĕd suuăs sjoolti moorằ, bắ qoodjăxi, baa qoodjăxi, maan-jærằcă, mar ă craainj, njïr aaci sjee tjee-tjïrjĕ căn talhu naa hælămoodj căn rooiv lesj nắ heegeeắlti (?), n' aaitj ă rằ rǫǫntji, mïắlti moorằ, llopïdaan acằs llapidaan, behi vĕăcă

bee-il djærăcă nă farigĕ ec eirji erj wuuesj acăs erj wasj ă
wadje ra̧a̧we ă djïĕna kool sjï acăs keluaj çooif feen; cur
eirji ăn ærigĕ nă tonni tjreeănă, sa̧a̧v lee sjï, sa̧a̧v lee cloori
cafi; lee meedj ăcăs lee bjræææxtje vï ă llonc ă sjoolu, cur
sjtrïqaalj sjï quuăn ăcăs'qalhu ĕstjæx cŏ Krjih-nă- Sorrăxă.''

The next is from "King Mananaun" (see page 67):—

"hlljeeăs sjï llonc woor-woxtăx woor-waxtăx cur aardi sjï
sjoolti mooră bă qoodjăxĕ baa qoodăxĕ xoo fadă xoo haardj
lee barră nă crænn, nær aac sjï tjee-tjïrje can brjisju, madje
ra̧a̧we căn reebu, llopidaan acăs llapidaan ec mïalti bĕăcă,
mïalti mooră nă farige hïr tjæ ext enjïr erj qos acăs bos a wadje
ra̧a̧we, cŏ duc sjï daa djrïĕn erj sjuul ăcăs tjrïĕn sqoodj, cŏ
ră nă æsconi ruuæædăli, quur enjïăxtăr doo ăcăs cannjiv in
uuăxtar, cŏ meerhitt sjï erj ă çï ruuă Wart dŏ vï rimpi acăs
năx meerhu ăn çi ruuă Wart vï nă djeei orhi; acăs dŏ vï sjï
sjoolu nï mï hol dŏ hænik sjï tælu.''

The third is from "The Champion of the Red Belt" (see
page 86):—

"Xŏ sjee amax ă hætă; rinn sjee llonc dŏ hæta, qrænn dŏ
wată, brată dŏ ljeeni. Hooc sjee hoolti, bŏqĕdje, baqĕdje, cŏ
baar nă crann djïrjĕ. Huc sjee oi-i erj mwirj acăs djerju lee
tjïrj, njïr aac sjee tjee-tjïrje căn brjisju noo qaabĕlĕ căn reebu,
cŏ ră sjee 'c ïsjtjæxt lee sjeetjvæ æx nă ro̧o̧ntji ăcăs geemnæx
nă beesjtji mooră, lee sjcrædi nă wilin; cŏ ro ïăsci bĕăcă
beelj djæric nă færige ec eerji erj hosj acăs erj wasj ă wadje
raawĕ, cur sjtjuur sjïăd seeăx stjæx fwï xuuirtj acăs xahirj rjï
Faahinj.''

Page 48. "The molten torrent," hile nă rïăxăn. The
translation is conjectural. From the context here something
fiery is evidently meant. The expression occurs again in
"King Mananaun" (page 74), where the narrator thought
something very cold was intended.

Page 64. "King Mananaun." The opening resembles a
story of Curtin's. Mananaun, the sea-god, was a great enchanter; hence, no doubt, the name of the King in this story.

Page 67. "The sea-run." See note to "Bioultach."

Page 68. "Faugauns and Blue-Men." The first word
appears to mean outlaws, and to be the origin of the word
"fachan" in the Scotch stories, which has hitherto not been
understood. Does Blue-men mean men stained with woad?

Page 74. "Nă riaxan." See note to "Bioultach," page 48.

Page 76. "Blauheen Blöye" appears to mean simply "smooth blossom." "The Amber Bracelet." Amber is not found in Ireland. It was formerly believed to have magical qualities. Pliny says, "True it is that a collar of amber beads worn about the necks of young infants is a singular preservative to them against secret poison, and a counter-charm for witchcraft and sorceries"; also, "The price of a small figure of it exceeds that of a healthy living slave."

Page 77. "Owas." The "owas" must be regarded as a distinct personage in Gaelic mythology. They appear to have been human in shape at least. They are met with several times in the Scotch stories, where the word is written "amhus," pronounced "owas." They have sometimes definite names, of which an example occurs a little farther on.

Page 78. "Criers" (of the kitchen). I am not sure this is the meaning of "clafirj." It may mean "gluttons."

Page 82. This makes the fourth time the hero is killed and revived.

Page 86. "The Champion of the Red Belt." The general tone of the story is wild and barbarous.

Page 86. "Providence." The Irish is "an rjï," a word frequently used in these Donegal stories in this sense.

Page 87. Lochlann is usually supposed to mean Denmark, but is by some held to be a purely mythical country.

Page 91. Another sea-run. See note to Bioultach.

Page 95. "Yard round the court." Yard is the word in the original; it means wall apparently. There are numbers of English words in this story, such as strain (of music), bride, cupboard, apron, destroy, alley playing ball, slaughter.

Page 100. The description of the hag corresponds closely with that of the "fachan" in the Scotch stories. It is interesting to compare the brief popular description of this monster with the laboured style of the written literature, as may be seen in the description of the hags in the "Cave of Keshcorran," Mr. S. H. O'Grady's "Silva Gadelica."

Page 106. The story of "Jack" has been given as a sample of the humorous story—quite different, it will be seen, from the style of Kennedy, or of any writer who uses "broken English." I have many others. I do not understand how they come so often to be called "Jack," as they are, in the Irish.

Page 107. Cleeve, an Irish word for basket.

Page 115. "The Servant of Poverty." This curious story, with its prosaic details, is chiefly remarkable for the variant it contains of the Cymbeline legend. A version much wilder than this is found in Campbell's "The Chest." The tale is thus seen to belong to the three kingdoms. A parallel to the opening incident of the betrothal of two children born at the same time will be found in the story of "The Wicked Greek Girl," given in Latin in "Silva Gadelica." Mr. O'Grady says it is not an Irish story.

Page 121. "Collegian." This is the word in the original, and seems to mean "a swell." The three sayings about bridge, house, and nag, also occur in Campbell's "Baillie Lunnain."

Page 125. "Covered the money"—*i.e.*, with her hand: accepted it.

Page 139. "The Son of the King of Prussia." Perhaps the most remarkable thing in this story is the name. I think if the tale had been written down twenty-five years ago, the name would not have occurred. I believe it to be not older than 1870. In that year Prussia was intensely unpopular in Ireland, owing to the sympathy felt for France ; and some one, perhaps M'Grale himself, took this method of showing his dislike for the former country by substituting this name for some other previously borne by the coward.

Page 149. "Crooked-mouth" is simply "Camp-bell," the order of adjective and noun—Beĕăl-qam—being reversed.

Page 152. "Bird-Serpent"—unique, I think.

Page 155. "Beauty of the World." There is nothing new except in some of the details in this story ; but the compact energy of the style is surely remarkable as coming from an unlettered peasant of eighty. Part of the story corresponds with the King of Ireland's son (Hyde's Collection). There is also a parallel in Curtin. With regard to the red, white, and black incident, it is worth noting that all primitive ideas of beauty depend on colour alone.

Page 156. "The red-haired young man" ought perhaps to be "the strong young man," in accordance with Mr. O'Grady's view.

Pages 160 and 164. "Part of milk and part of blood." The full meaning is "one-third of milk, one-third of blood, and one-third of urine."

Page 168. What the meaning of this strange tale may be I cannot conjecture. It is either an allegory—the name "Grig" (gruig) signifies churlishness—or it is a fragment of a rather ghastly piece of mythology. Several things in the translation are conjectural; for the Irish is full of difficulties, as the narrator, before I began to write, warned me would be the case.

Page 172. "Cornelius" is a translation of despair. The Irish is "qornjili."

Page 173. The word translated "hellebore" is "dææhooh."

Page 174. This little tale has a close parallel in Grimm, which is why I have printed it. There is also a version in Kennedy

Page 179. The end of the story is like Kennedy's "Twelve Wild Geese," and it has also a close parallel in Grimm. But all the earlier portion has no parallel in either.

Page 187. The names of the three brothers are a little puzzling, as "Inn" seems to be only the aspirated form—the vocative of Fionn which means fair, white; while Glégil means Clear-Bright.

Page 188. This touching tale has a curious far-away resemblance to certain classic legends. A good deal must be lost, and in consequence the long struggle of the young man with the devil has much that requires explanation. It is unique among Celtic stories.

Page 196. "The Djachwi." I am not sure that this word is anything more than "drachmhadh," a tithe, which has been turned into a person, the meaning being forgotten. After the briefly told Andromeda episode the story takes a quite novel turn. Its resemblance in structure, as is the case also with some of the other stories, to many a modern novel is very apparent.

Page 203. "The skin of the wild pig." The Irish of the two last words is "mwike tuusjke." I am doubtful as to the translation which was given by M'Ginty. In the story of the "Fate of the Children of Tuireann," one of the tasks imposed on the three brothers is to obtain the skin of a pig having marvellous qualities, which has to be taken from the King of Greece, whose name is Tuis. There appears to be some connection.

Page 211. "The Red Pony." The word translated pony

is, in this tale, "klebisjtjïn"; in the preceding tale it is
"plebisjtjïn." Wonderful "horse-beasts" thus occur four
times in this volume. In two stories it will be noted that they
are merely human beings, enchanted ; in the other two this is
apparently not the case. The word rendered "healing water"
is, in this, as in all the other stories in which it occurs,
"ïqlæntj" (Donegal pron.), which literally means, "cure-
health."

Page 219. "The Nine-legged Steed." The opening resembles a story of Curtin's, in which, however, the step-mother
acts from the motive of hate instead of, as here, from affection.
The words translated "transforming caps" are "qahal"
(cochal), which also means a cloak, and "qantræltje," the
translation of which is a guess. It must be inferred that of
the three maidens, who came as swans, one was the nine-
legged steed, another the lady in the greenawn. The third
is not accounted for. "Greenawn" (griänaan) means "sunny
chamber." In Irish tales the ladies are generally described
as occupying such apartments; a more general use of the
word is found on page 179.

THE END.

Elliot Stock, 62, Paternoster Row, London.